D1642537

STORM DOGS

Annabel Claridge was born in 1955.
Her working background is in journalism and design.
When her poodle, Bo, barked at a stuffed King Charles
spaniel in a glass case, the idea was sparked for a series of
adventure stories about a modern-day poodle, an ancient
spaniel and their friendship in past lives.

The court of King Charles I seemed the obvious setting
for the first book, and Annabel began her research for
STORM DOGS. One of the first things she discovered
was that the king's cavalry commander, Prince Rupert,
had a poodle too. His name was Boy, and he used to ride
into battle on the front of his master's saddle.

Still more coincidences were to come, and Annabel
now writes Bo's adventures full-time from her home in
Somerset.

STORM DOGS

Annabel Claridge

Hemington Publishing

First published in 2008
by Hemington Publishing Limited
18 Magdalens Road, Ripon, HG4 1HX

www.hemingtonpublishing.co.uk

ISBN 978-0-9558142-0-4

Printed in Great Britain
A CIP catalogue record is available for this book from
The British Library

For John Claridge
1926-2006

The following story is based on actual events

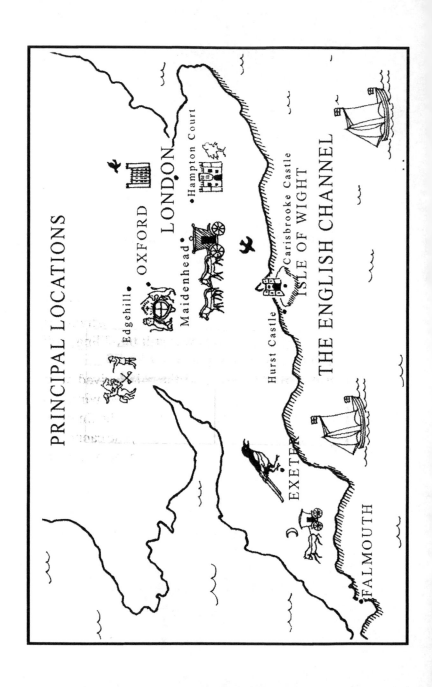

PRINCIPAL LOCATIONS

CHAPTER ONE
Bo's House, somewhere in England.
The 21st Century

Bo knew the storm was coming, she felt it in her bones. She paced the floor in dread until she heard the first roll of thunder. Then she lowered her tail and crawled under the kitchen table. She found a piece of cheese and nibbled at it desperately. She hoped it would distract her from her fear, but it didn't. She was still trembling, still alone in the house.

The storm moved closer, and the rain arrived with a vengeance. It drummed against the kitchen windows and rattled the glass, but it could not drown the thunder. When a furious clap broke over Bo's head, she cannoned out from under the table and raced towards the one place the storm couldn't reach.

She paused to glance at the clock in the hall, then pushed open the door to the cellar, padded down its stone steps, and stopped. The cellar wasn't as dark as usual. A band of light was shining low down on its far side. It was seeping out from under a door, a door she'd never seen before. She lowered her head and crept forward until she was within reach of the door and could nudge at it with her paw. It creaked open and she blinked in the sudden brightness.

She was standing on the threshold of a small room. It was flooded with light, but when she checked the ceiling for a fluorescent tube, or at the very least a light bulb, she saw nothing there. There *was* a skylight, but its smooth glass was as black as the night outside. The bricks in the wall beside her were black, too. They had a bitter-sweet smell, like charred wood, and were twinkling with tiny particles of glittering dust. In times past, this room had been a coal hole.

In those days, the house had had many fires and stoves to fuel, and the coal had been delivered through a trap door and poured down a chute to be stored here. Now, though, the house had central heating, the trap door and chute had become a skylight, and the room was redundant. It was also very bare, except for some tins of old paint in one corner, and a heap of folded dust sheets in another.

Bo had just turned to walk away when she heard a shuffling sound behind her. She whipped round and saw the dust sheets topple sideways. More shuffling, and one of the sheets began to rise and fall as if it were breathing. Bo's heart pounded in her chest. She thought she should probably run for her life, but she was too spellbound to move. She watched, transfixed, as the sheet fluttered and heaved and something stepped out of it. Now she *really* wanted to run but, as the sheet collapsed to the ground with a sigh, she realised she couldn't move. Her legs had disconnected from her brain, and there was nothing she could do about it.

The something edged towards her. Its feet scraped on the floor, shrivelled and squirrel-like. Its raised head had a cracked, leathery nose, and eyes that, though round and brown, were as expressionless as glass.

'Go away! Go away!' Bo barked.

She knew the creature understood. She knew it was a fellow dog, but it ignored her.

It took another step and clumps of its fur fell away, revealing patches of grey, wrinkled skin. The clumps hit the ground and disintegrated into brittle hairs yet, even as they rose and danced in the air, the dog's horrific appearance began to fade. The bald patches plumped up and turned a healthy pink. A glossy new chestnut-and-white coat began to form, and the withered tail became a glorious, wagging curtain. Now Bo could see that the dog was a type of spaniel. Its noble head and luxurious ears reminded her of a Cavalier King Charles.

'Who are you?' she asked. 'Are you real?'

She felt much calmer now. She was no longer paralysed with fear. She thought she might even be able to run if she wanted to, but she didn't.

'Why don't you touch me and see?' the dog answered.

Bo reached out a paw and swiftly snatched it back.

'Touch me,' the spaniel repeated.

Bo reached again, hesitated, and lowered her paw. The spaniel's coat was warm and silky. She pressed into it more firmly, but as she did so she felt a strange sensation in her hind legs. She glanced down at the floor and saw that it had spun itself into an inverted cone. Now it was tugging at her ankles as if trying to suck her in. She tried to leap away but discovered she'd been wrong to think she could run whenever she wanted. Her limbs still wouldn't work. She yelped and turned to the spaniel for help.

'What's happening?' she barked.

'Something wonderful,' the spaniel replied. 'Something very wonderful. Let it take you where it will. Don't fight it, Bo. Don't fi...'

As the spaniel's voice faded into a distant gurgle, Bo felt herself tumble and whirr. She wanted to be terrified. She wanted to shudder and tremble, to squeal and howl, if only because it might make her feel real again. Yet somehow she knew she *was* real. She still existed. She still had bone and muscle, a pumping heart and flowing blood. Her curly black fur, boot button eyes and long, triangular ears were still there, as was the pompom on the end of her tail.

She was still a poodle, still Bo.

As far as she could tell, she was in a current of warm air, her own mini tornado. Then she saw that she wasn't alone. Other things were spinning too, though she was moving too fast to see what they were.

The spinning slowed until it was no more than a gentle current and Bo found she could float about. Her ears streamed out behind her whilst she steered and doggy-paddled with her feet, and she began to see that the other things were small black poodles, just like her. Some came so close that she could almost touch them, but they didn't acknowledge her, nor she them. They *seemed* real, but also not.

Then, quite suddenly, one poodle swam right up to her and looked her in the eye. Bo raised a paw, and the poodle raised its opposite paw. Bo tipped her head to the right, and the poodle tipped its head to the left. Everything Bo did, the other poodle did too, at exactly the same time, and in exactly the same manner, but in the opposite way, as though Bo was watching her own reflection.

But Bo knew what she looked like, and this poodle wasn't her.

Until then, its gaze had remained fixed and unblinking. Now it closed its eyes slowly and deliberately, like an owl, and, unable to stop herself, Bo closed *her* eyes, too.

When she opened them again, the strange poodle and its watery world had gone, and Bo was somewhere else entirely.

CHAPTER TWO

The Palace of Whitehall, London, England.
Summer 1639

She was sitting on a lady's knee at a wide, polished table. In front of her was a bowl of heart-shaped biscuits. She knew the biscuits were intended for her, but she couldn't reach them. She could barely move her head.

Her collar was magnificent, and wildly impractical. It was decorated with rows and rows of drop pearls, and these irritating, dangling baubles had snagged in her ears. She'd twisted and wriggled and strived to pull them off with her teeth, but she'd only managed to make things worse.

The lady tutted and tried to tease the pearls free. Her hands were small and white and her bracelets tinkled whilst she worked at the snags.

Finally, she sighed in defeat and addressed a man seated on the far side of the table.

'We do not like these pearls, Monsieur,' she told him with a French accent.

'No, we do not,' mumbled Bo.

'They are too long,' the lady added.

The man, who had long dark hair, a short, pointed

beard and a moustache, raised his eyebrows.

'Then have the jeweller remove them, dear,' he suggested patiently.

'And what shall we have instead?' asked the lady.

She swivelled Bo towards a young boy. He was spearing strawberries with a gold fork and had spattered the front of his jacket with tiny spots of pink juice. He had grubby fingernails, food around his mouth, and unbrushed hair that stuck up in tufts all over his head.

'Consider her costume, Charles,' he was told. 'What think you?'

The boy gave his opinion with a bored sigh.

'The pearls are too long, maman,' he said. 'I prefer emeralds. Emeralds will suit her very well.'

Bo was swivelled again, this time towards a girl, but, whilst her head and body moved obligingly enough, her eyes remained fixed on the man, who was now breaking lumps from a hunk of bread and spooning a steaming dark broth to his mouth.

She sniffed the air.

'Venison potage,' she noted, much to her surprise.

She'd never heard of venison, or potage.

'With cabbage and peas,' she added.

The man dabbed at his moustache with a napkin, then broke another piece of bread and swirled it around in his dish until it was soaked with the rich, delicious soup. He raised his hand towards his mouth, hesitated, and then lowered the gravy-soaked morsel to his lap. Bo watched, fascinated, as the head of a spaniel appeared above the level of the table and took the bread. Its eyes glazed

over with pleasure, and Bo swore.

'Rats!'

'Mary?' the lady asked the girl. 'What is your idea for the collar. Shall we have the pearls replaced?'

'We should, maman,' Mary replied. 'Have the jeweller remove them, but set diamonds in their stead. Diamonds are sweeter than emeralds, and they sparkle so prettily against her fur.'

'Good answer,' thought Bo.

She tilted her nose.

'Funny smell,' she muttered. 'Not venison potage. Not cabbage, not peas. Something else. Something so... so...'

She sneezed, 'Ha...ha...choo!' and the lady stroked her back and pointed to a portrait on the wall.

'Hush,' she said softly. ''Tis only our new painting that makes you sneeze. It is done with oils, you see. The smell will fade in time. It is pretty, don't you think? Our Majesties are certainly very taken with it. Do you see how handsome our children are? I think the likeness of Charles especially good.'

Bo studied the portrait carefully and realised that some of its subjects were sitting right there at the table. She recognised the girl called Mary, the boy Charles, and the spaniel. There were three other children in the painting too, but Charles was the central figure. He was immaculately dressed and very clean, and was standing with his hand resting on the head of a second dog, a mastiff. It was the size of a small pony.

'So. We have decided on diamonds,' the lady

announced as she unfastened Bo's collar and laid it on the table. 'Now, chérie, it is time for your morning walk.'

She beckoned to a man who'd been standing discreetly in the background and he stepped forward, lifted Bo up and carried her out of the room, across a panelled hallway, and into a garden.

The man set Bo down on a path, and the pony dog from the portrait ambled towards them.

'Yer uz be,' the man said. ''Ee can croopy now, cassen thee. Look, 'ere's comp'ny for thee.'

'*What* did he say?' the pony dog asked. 'I can't make out his dialect.'

Bo shook her head.

'Me neither,' she said.

'Oh well,' the dog replied, 'it's only his second day in the job. I dare say we'll get attuned to him, eventually. I have managed to learn his name, though.'

'Oh?'

'Edmund Smales, they call him. Where's Cavendish?'

'Who?' asked Bo.

The pony dog seemed to think this a very witty remark and laughed long and hard.

'Very droll,' he wheezed. 'Let's disown him! After all, he never comes for walks with us nowadays. He's always too busy lazing on our master's knee, savouring soup and...other...scrumptious...morsels.'

The dog shook his jowls and slobbered all over Bo,

who suddenly realised who Cavendish was.

'He's been having his potage,' she said.

'Mutton?' the pony dog drooled.

'No,' Bo replied. 'Venison.'

'Oh, lucky, lucky boy.'

'My thoughts exactly,' agreed Bo.

The two dogs meandered companionably along the path, and Bo examined the garden. It wasn't at all how she expected a garden to be. There were no borders of colourful plants, no ivy-covered walls, no swings or slides or patio furniture. It was all very neat and regimented and carefully divided by miniature clipped hedges. All the bushes were manicured into obelisks and globes, and even the roses and herbs seemed to be standing to attention.

She heard the sound of a little girl's laughter and stood on her hind legs.

'That's Mary,' she muttered as she recognised the girl who'd voted for diamonds. 'With a toddler. And a gardener.'

She glanced over her shoulder.

Edmund Smales was right on her heels.

'Do distract him for me,' she asked the pony dog. 'I'm going to see Mary.'

'Old Sowerbutts the gardener, more like!' the dog teased. 'But I'll oblige.'

He did this by barking loudly and making a sudden, slightly arthritic rush at something imaginary. When Smales turned to see what was up, Bo took her chance and bounced over the little hedges to where Mary was patiently playing bat and ball with her baby sister, Elizabeth.

The little girls greeted Bo with shrieks, giggles and pleas for her to join their game, but she ignored them. The pony dog had been right. The old gardener was much more appealing. He had a fluffy white beard and a big straw hat, but what really intrigued Bo was his buff leather apron.

She rushed up to him.

'Mornin'!' he called cheerily. 'Run away from that new footman have you? Good for you.'

He slid his hand over the apron and delved deep into a pocket on its front.

'Here y'are,' he said.

He handed Bo a soily biscuit.

She ate it, and another, and then lay down on the warm grass to sleep.

She'd enjoyed her dream, but she hoped it would end now. She wanted to wake up on her bed at home, where the thunderstorm would have passed, there'd be no weird spaniel in the cellar, and she could watch breakfast TV.

CHAPTER THREE
Bo's House.
The 21st Century

A bright white light switched on in Bo's brain and she opened her eyes. She was back home, all right, but not in bed, as she'd wanted to be. She was still in the coal hole, still standing with her paw on the spaniel's shoulder.

'Ugh,' she groaned.

She lifted the paw, placed it on the ground and shook herself.

'Bbrrr-gug-gug-gug, I'm dreaming and I want to wake *up,* hah!'

It was a spectacular shake, but it changed nothing. When she finally stopped shuddering, the spaniel and the bright light were still there.

'You're not dreaming,' the spaniel replied. 'You never were. I told you something wonderful was happening. Everything you did and saw was real.'

Bo ignored him.

'I dreamt I was sitting on a lady's knee,' she said. 'She was asking everyone what could be done about my collar.'

'Did you see a spaniel?'

'Yes! A man was feeding it with venison potage.'

'I was that spaniel.'

Bo took no notice and rambled on.

'There was a painting as well, in the *dream*,' she raised her voice insistently. 'It smelled funny and made me sneeze. It was hanging on the wall behind the man. His spaniel was in it.'

'I know it well,' the spaniel replied in his quiet way. 'Personally speaking, I never thought my likeness a very good one, though I probably shouldn't say that. The chap who did it was the greatest portrait painter of his day. His name was Anthony Van Dyck and there are many books about him. You might even find that very painting in one of them, if you had a mind.'

'Pah!' Bo guffawed. 'How could something from a dream be in a book?'

'Quite,' said the spaniel.

He paused to brush a paw across his face as if trying to suppress a smile.

'To your right is a stack of paint tins,' he continued, 'one of them has a blue label...'

'I see it,' said Bo.

'Then watch closely. In two seconds precisely, a spider will cross the top of that tin and drop to the floor.'

Bo watched as, sure enough, two spidery legs appeared and groped for purchase on the tin's slippery lid. The rest of the spider followed, scuttled across the lid, and dropped.

'How did you...?' Bo began, but just then, an identical spider appeared at exactly the same spot on the edge of the same tin.

'Is there a nest of those things?'

'No. It's the same spider.'

'But I've seen him three times already! And there he is again! Why does he keep doing that?'

'He doesn't. He's done it only once. What you are seeing is a *replay*.'

Bo scratched an ear.

'I don't understand,' she said.

'No? Well, that's hardly surprising. To put it simply, your coming here and discovering me has altered the pattern of time. The time you live in has all but stopped. I say "all but" because time must always tick over. If it ever stopped completely, the world would end. So, in circumstances such as this, it replays the last two seconds of itself. Hence the spider.'

'So could he do that forever?'

'No,' the spaniel chuckled. 'There is no forever without time. The spider is merely locked in a moment. As soon as you leave the cellar, that moment will pass and time and the spider will move on.'

'You mean I'll wake up from my dream? Because I think I *should*, you know. I've been dreaming for *ages*.'

'There is no dream. I thought I'd explained that. You can't wake up because you are not asleep. And ages don't come into it. There can be no ages, without time.'

'Oh,' said Bo lamely. 'Still, I'd better go. It was very nice to dream you but I'm going to wake up now.'

She raised a paw.

'Bye, then,' she whispered.

15

'Bye,' the spaniel sighed.

Bo didn't look back until she'd reached the other side of the cellar. When she did, the coal hole was still blazing with light and the spaniel was still sitting in its centre.

She climbed the cellar steps, pushed open the door to the hall, then turned and looked again. She could no longer see the coal hole, but she could tell that the light had gone out. The rest of the house was just as she'd left it. There was still thunder overhead and it was still raining. She studied the clock in the hall. Its hands hadn't moved but neither had it stopped. Bo could hear it ticking. She wasn't sure what that meant, but then she didn't really need to know. Instinct told her that everything that had happened since she'd entered the cellar had taken no time at all.

CHAPTER FOUR
A little later

Later that night, Bo lay on the bed and thought about her strange dream.

'What I don't understand,' she muttered to herself, 'is where I fell asleep in the first place. Not in the kitchen, obviously. I could never have fallen asleep *there*, not in the middle of a storm.'

She sat up and scratched an ear.

'So it must have been in the cellar,' she concluded. 'And if everything after that was a dream, then the little room with the glass ceiling was part of that dream. Which must mean it doesn't exist. And now I shall have to find out,' she huffed, 'because I shan't sleep again until I do.'

She slipped off the bed and trotted downstairs to the hall where she pushed open the door to the cellar and paused. She was having second thoughts. It was the middle of the night, after all. Maybe she should wait until morning. Someone was bound to go into the cellar at some point and she could go with them.

On the other hand, she could just take things one step at a time. If she didn't like it, she could turn around and come straight back.

She started tenuously, but the further she went the more light there was. When she reached the coal hole for the second time that day, the spaniel was already there.

'Hello again,' it said.

'Who *are* you?' Bo asked from a distance.

'You were thinking of me,' the spaniel replied. 'That's nice.'

'No I wasn't,' Bo snapped defensively.

'You've done it again, Bo. You've put present time on hold.'

'No I haven't. I'm just having another dream.'

'Do you always dream this much?'

Bo shook her head.

'No,' she said, 'it must be the cheese. I found it under the kitchen table.'

'You like cheese, do you? Mignonne liked cheese.'

'Meen-yong,' Bo repeated. 'What's that?'

'French.'

'I don't speak French. What does it mean?'

'Dainty, cute. It was your name, once.'

'No it wasn't. My name's Bo.'

'In this life, yes,' the spaniel agreed. 'But in another life it was Mignonne. You wore a drop pearl collar, remember? And a spaniel was being fed with venison potage.'

'That *was* a dream.'

The spaniel sighed and waved a paw in the general direction of the hall.

'Very well,' he said wearily. 'Go on then, go back to

bed.'

Bo stayed where she was.

'Lesson one,' the spaniel suddenly declared, 'is that you must listen. Lesson two is that you must trust. Lesson three is that you must believe. Learn those three things, and you will know that these experiences are not dreams. You will be able to visit another world. Think about it. You can come and see me anytime, I'm always here.'

'Another world?' Bo asked.

'Mignonne's world,' the spaniel replied.

Bo took a step forward.

'Believe what?'

'That you are not dreaming, that present time is on hold whilst we are together, and that you really were Mignonne.'

'It's hard,' said Bo.

'The best things often are.'

'Will you show me what to do?'

'Of course I will,' answered the spaniel kindly. 'First you must come here and put your paw on my shoulder. Just like the last time. Good. Now try to imagine a very grand house. It has a large entrance hall with a chequered marble floor. I'll tell you more when you return.'

'Hold on a sec',' said Bo. 'Return *how*? And from *where*?'

'Leave all that to me,' the spaniel said. 'Now think of the grand house, the hall...'

Bo felt nothing untoward this time.

There was nothing to warn or prepare her.

She was taken completely unawares by what happened

next.

CHAPTER FIVE

The home of Sir Anthony Van Dyck,
Blackfriars, London.
Autumn 1641

She was trotting across a grand entrance hall. There was a sweeping staircase ahead of her and several panelled and gilded doorways to her left and right.

Beside her, gold taffeta skirts rocked backwards and forwards, satin heels clacked on the floor, and she caught a glimpse of sparkling diamond shoe-buckles.

She glanced up and saw the lady whose knee she'd been sitting on in her dream. She recognised the face with its glittering brown eyes, broad smile and slightly buck teeth. The scent was familiar, too, a subtle blend of silk, powder and perfume.

But there was another, much less subtle scent in the air.

'I know that smell,' muttered Bo, 'though I can't think why. It's pungent and disgusting.'

She felt a tickling sensation in her nose and stopped.

She made a little snorting noise to clear her head, but the tickle got worse and she sneezed.

'Haa...ha...choo!'

The lady hovered patiently whilst another lady, a lady-in-waiting, stepped forward and dabbed at Bo's nose with a square of silk.

'Now return to the carriage,' said Bo's lady coolly. 'And take the guards with you.'

Bo hadn't noticed the guards. They'd been following at a respectful distance, but since everyone had come to a standstill, they'd caught up. And they didn't seem too keen to leave.

'Your Majesty...' one of them protested.

Bo's lady sighed.

'Crauford,' she replied. 'Remove yourself. I will be moments only. What can happen to us in this house of a dear friend?'

Crauford nodded. He knew that his charges were safe, but it was still his duty to protect them.

He tried again.

'His Majesty has given clear instructions,' he said.

'Oh very well!' huffed the lady. 'But you can wait here, in the hall. Come, Mignonne.'

Bo remembered the word Mignonne. The spaniel had told her it had been her name, once. The lady seemed to think so too, and when she strode forth again, Bo high-stepped proudly beside her.

They approached a pair of double doors. A man was standing beside them, and Bo realised that he was dressed in a very similar way to Edmund Smales, the man who'd taken her and the pony dog for a walk. At the time, it hadn't occurred to Bo that Smales might be rather overdressed for the task. She'd been too absorbed in other things. Now, though, and as the footman reached out and opened the doors with a flourish, she took note of his multi-buttoned coat, his silk breeches and stockings and, most glamorous of all, the ribbon rosettes on the front of his shoes.

Bo and the lady swept into a large, sunlit room.

It was inhabited by a group of gentlemen, guests of the house's owner. They were lolling about and drinking wine, and Bo's new eye for fashion told her that they were very flamboyantly clothed. She was still staring at their expensive silks, brocades and braids when they put down their drinks, got to their feet, and bowed.

Bo reeled, and sneezed again.

The hall had smelled of roses compared to this place. The stench was overpowering, a heady cocktail of oil, chalk and soot.

One of the men walked boldly forward and took Bo's lady's hand in his. Unlike the other gentlemen, he was dressed down and mostly in black except for a pale linen smock which was smeared with ancient stains and daubs of paint. His hair was loose, curly and reddish-brown, and he had a startlingly red moustache.

'Your Majesty,' he said, bending to kiss the lady's ringed fingers, 'and little Mignonne.'

He paused.

'May I?' he asked.

'But of course!' the lady replied. 'Is that not why we are here? Mignonne? This is Monsieur Anthony Van Dyck.'

The fumes in the room were making Bo queasy, now, and she was desperate for water and air. She could sense the other men staring at her. They kept cupping their hands and whispering. Every so often one of them laughed. When Monsieur Anthony leant towards her and his red moustache twitched in her face, it was the final straw.

She wanted to go home.

She yelped and ran.

'Stop her!' cried the lady.

'Guards!' shouted Monsieur Anthony.

Bo shot past the footman and back through the double doors. She skated across the chequered marble floor, heading for the front door but, just as she was nearing it, two guards knelt down and crossed their swords to block her way. She braked hard, skidded on her bottom, and came to an inelegant halt.

The swords' lethal blades were right in front of her nose.

She struggled to her feet and turned to run in another direction. She could see an open doorway on the far side of the hall and began to make for it. More guards appeared. She squealed, raced to the bottom of the staircase and charged up its sweeping curve.

Halfway there she stopped, poked her head between two of the gilded balusters, and looked down.

Below her were Monsieur Anthony and the lady.

'Please come down,' the lady called.

Bo withdrew her head, shook it, and climbed two more steps.

She was beginning to feel a bit foolish. She knew there was no escape but she was determined not to give in. She considered lying down. If only she could fall asleep, she might wake up at home. Yet if she did lie down, she'd almost certainly be caught. Just then, there was a soft tread beside her and someone knelt to stroke her back.

'They don't mean you no 'arm,' said a young voice. 'That I do know. All they want's your portrait done by my master. And he is the greatest painter of the day, I do say.'

The boy slipped his hand under her chest and lifted her gently into his arms.

'It is a great honour to be painted by him, Mignonne,' he explained gently. 'An' so you must sit for him, an' let him paint a pretty picture of you. For you is surely the most pretty and most famous dog in England, and therefore it should be done by him, I do say.'

He carried Bo down the flight of stairs and entered the room to the sound of cheers.

'Gentlemen,' Mr Van Dyck addressed his guests when they'd stopped applauding. 'I must bid you an early farewell, for there is work to be done and my subject is too nervous for your audience.'

The men picked up their hats and cloaks agreeably, and came forward to kiss Bo's lady's hand. They exchanged a few words with her and their host, and then left the room.

When the last of them had gone, Mr Van Dyck knelt beside Bo, took her lower jaw in one hand, and turned her head gently from side to side to catch the light from the room's many tall windows.

'Perfect,' he said.

Bo was beginning to like Mr Van Dyck.

She was even getting used to the room's strange smells.

The painter stood up and clapped his hands.

'Charcoal black, lead white, lead-tin yellow!' he called. 'Oh, and een beetje red - carmine, perhaps?'

It all sounded like double Dutch to Bo, but whilst she'd been out of the room, two young men had arrived. They seemed to understand exactly what Van Dyck had said, and now set about their business.

In front of them was a huge wooden workbench.

Lined along it was an orderly row of glass-stoppered jars, perhaps twenty or more, each one filled with a different, brightly-coloured powder. Behind these came an array of pots of various sizes, small ones with lids, and big ones stuffed with clumps of well-used paintbrushes. There were pestles and mortars too, and many bottles and beakers, stoneware ewers and piles of oily rags.

The young men rolled up their sleeves, selected some of the coloured powders, and poured pyramids of them onto marble slabs. To this they added dollops of linseed oil, which they mixed well in with fat wooden pestles.

'Now then, Mignonne,' Mr Van Dyck said gently.

He picked Bo up and carried her to the other side of the room, where he set her down on a chair. Behind it was a length of pink silk, which had been pinned to the wall and arranged in folds to make a fetching backdrop.

'The collar?' Mr Van Dyck inquired.

Bo's lady nodded and then motioned to the footman, who slipped out of the room and returned with the lady-in-waiting.

She was carrying an embroidered box with an arched lid, gold handles and a mother-of-pearl keyhole. She curtsied, laid the box on a table, and produced two golden keys from a ribbon at her waist.

She unlocked the box with one of the keys, folded back its lid, and inserted the second key into its side, whereupon the box's front sprang open. Inside it were three trays. She pulled a little tab and the mechanism's clever hinges concertinaed all the trays out, like a flight of steps. Carefully arranged on each level were three glittering dog collars.

Bo gasped and craned her neck.

'What think you, Monsieur Anthony?' her lady asked. 'You must choose.'

Mr Van Dyck stepped forward, perused the collars and removed two of them. He strode over to Bo and held the first collar against her chest. It was a broad band set with five rows of pearls.

'Charming,' he said, rubbing the side of his nose pensively.

Bo glanced down at the shimmering beads.

'*Charming*?' she muttered. 'Is that the best you can do?'

'But no,' said Van Dyck.

'No?'

'Not enough colour. Black dog. White pearls.'

'True...'

Van Dyck tossed the collar aside and held out his other choice. This was more like a necklace than a collar, and was only really for sitting still in, otherwise it could fall over a dog's head or get tangled up in its feet. It was a strand of aquamarines interspersed with diamonds.

'That'll do fine,' mumbled Bo.

'This one. This one is perfect,' Van Dyck declared.

He lowered the necklace over Bo's head and fastened its clasp. Then he adjusted its fall and carefully repositioned any stones that had got buried in fur.

By now the young men, who were the painter's apprentices, had finished their mixing and stepped away from the bench. Each carried a palette of the oil paints they'd just prepared, and a fistful of brushes of varying length and thickness.

Mr Van Dyck turned to Bo's lady.

'Your Majesty will stay and watch?' he asked, clearly hoping she wouldn't.

'Non, non,' the lady replied tactfully, 'I must leave you in peace.'

She patted Bo's head.

'Alors, ma petite,' she said. 'Sit nicely for your portrait, and when Mr Van Dyck is ready he will send you home in his carriage.'

She bid good-bye to the painter, blew a kiss to Bo, and turned to the footman.

'Tell the kitchens to bring a saucer of milk at two o'clock precisely, and a slice of ripe cheese at four,' she said.

Then she swept out of the room, taking the lady-in-waiting and the box of rejected collars with her.

When she'd gone, one of the assistants carried an easel across the floor, set it down in front of Bo, and placed a canvas upon it.

'So! We begin!' Mr Van Dyck announced. 'You must sit very still now, Mignonne.'

CHAPTER SIX
A few minutes later

Bo found it hard to keep still at the best of times, so holding a pose for her portrait was very hard indeed. But she'd come to like Mr Van Dyck with his red moustache and his strong-smelling paints, and when her milk and cheese arrived at the appointed times she ignored them.

Finally, the painter said he'd done enough for that day, and Bo was relieved to be able to move, though in two minds about going home.

'Because I *am* going home, obviously. In a moment I shall wake up, or whatever it is I need to do. Though it's been very nice here, I must say.'

She jumped stiffly from her chair and trotted round to the front of the easel to see the portrait's progress so far, but the canvas had already been covered.

'You cannot see it yet, Mignonne,' said Van Dyck from over her shoulder. 'That is a rule. All portraits must be finished before they are seen by their subjects. But come, look at this one instead.'

He strode across the room, picked up a different painting, and propped it against the wall.

It featured a boy. He appeared to be about twelve

years old, and was wearing black breeches, a matching jacket, and a stiff white collar and cuffs. Hanging from his side was a very grown-up-looking sword, clearly no toy, and sitting on the ground, looking adoringly up at him, was a large, pale-coloured hound.

'You like it?' Mr Van Dyck inquired.

Bo tipped her head.

'Yes,' she thought. 'I do. He looks a little arrogant for someone so young, and I'm not sure he should be carrying a sword at his age. But he's clearly a dog-lover so, yes, I like it.'

'He is the king's nephew, Prince Rupert von der Pfalz,' Van Dyck explained. 'He sat for this portrait nine years ago, now, so he looks very different these days. He is no longer the shy boy you see here, but a brave and beautiful young man.'

At that moment the door opened and the footman stepped into the room and announced that Bo's carriage awaited.

The painter knelt down to remove the aquamarine and diamond collar.

'Couldn't I keep that?' Bo wondered.

But no, the clasp was already undone.

'I will store it safely,' said Van Dyck as he folded his fist around the collar. 'We will need it for your next sitting.'

Bo cocked her head quizzically.

'It takes many hours to complete a great portrait, Mignonne. I will do what I can without you, but you must come again. And soon, I hope.'

He rolled into a sitting position and lowered his voice.

'Perhaps by then Prince Rupert will be here,' he murmured. 'He is abroad now, but I expect him to return soon.'

Bo wagged her tail at the prospect of meeting a real life, brave and beautiful prince, but Van Dyck shook his head sadly and made a tutting noise.

'It will not be a good sign. Already one has to be careful what one says. Mark my words, a storm is brewing. And when it comes, Prince Rupert will come, too.'

Bo stared at the painter and stretched a paw towards him. She had no idea what he was talking about. He took her paw in one hand and tugged affectionately at her ears.

'I fear there are unhappy times ahead, Mignonne,' he sighed. 'But you are too beautiful to worry about such things. Too beautiful and far too innocent.'

He let go of Bo and rose to his feet.

'Take care of your beauty and innocence, Mignonne, and be of comfort to your mistress. She will need your friendship in the days to come. So!' he added more cheerfully. 'I'll see you soon for another sitting. Vaarwel, Mignonne!'

Bo trotted out of the studio and followed the footman across the chequered hall and out into the low afternoon sun, where she stopped dead in her tracks.

'What on earth's *that*?' she asked herself. 'It looks

like a Christmas pudding.'

Anthony Van Dyck's coach was actually a rather grand affair, by the standards of the day. It was made of gilded leather stretched over a wooden frame, and had a team of horses to pull it, and four very large wheels. A pageboy was standing proudly beside it, and Bo recognised him as the boy who'd picked her up on the staircase.

He was dressed like a mini-footman and was slightly built with a shock of dark, floppy hair and extraordinary, pale-grey eyes.

Bo clambered up the coach steps and the pageboy climbed in beside her, closed the blinds and sat down.

'I am to 'comp'ny you home,' he said proudly. 'To St. James's Palace! I shall tell my ma and pa when I do see them next, I shall. I shall say that I did escort the queen's most precious pet. A poodle, that is, whose name is Mignonne.'

He leant forward and kissed Bo's head.

'And I shall tell them,' he continued as the coach moved forward and he wrapped his arms around Bo's neck, 'that I have kissed a head which has surely been kissed by our dear queen, who has no doubt kissed the king himself! And that is information what will please my ma and pa very much, I do ...'

Bo hadn't heard what the pageboy was saying. Her ears had been tuned in to something else entirely. The sound had been distant at first but had gradually got closer and louder. Now she could hear it quite distinctly, even over the rattling of the coach's wheels and the clip-clop of its horses' hooves.

She sat up sharply.

'What's that?' the pageboy asked. 'D'you hear it too?'

The commotion seemed to have reached the very street where they were making slow progress through traffic. Now Bo could make out individual voices.

'No popery!' shouted one.

'No finery!' yelled another.

Bo nudged at the window blind with her nose, hoping to make it spring open. As she did so, something hit its outer side with a crack and a splat. She watched, fascinated, whilst the contents of a rotten egg slithered down the blind and dripped onto the window frame beside her. She flinched and flared her nostrils at the stench of ammonia, and another, equally rotten egg, opened with a pop against the coach's door.

'Down with the queen!'

'No to the brat of France!'

'Send the harlot home!'

The pageboy grabbed Bo by the scruff of her neck.

'Quick,' he hissed urgently. 'Stay down an' you'll be safe! Remember they's don't know you are here, for this coach belongs to Van Dyck, and not to Her Majesty, praise be.'

He pushed Bo roughly off his knee and onto the floor. Then he reached across the seat, shook open a travel rug and threw it over her head.

Bo lay as flat as she could.

She could hear the horses whinnying in fear.

'Stand back!' the coachman kept shouting. 'Stand back!'

Bo pressed her every muscle hard against the floor as the coach jolted and lurched its way through a barrage of flying missiles. She stayed like that, trembling and panting, for what seemed an age, but finally the noise receded and the pageboy leant forward and peered at her from between his stockinged legs.

''Tis all safe now,' he said. 'Come up, Mignonne, an' sit with me the last stretch.'

He pulled a cord, and the egg-stained blind rolled up to reveal a golden autumn evening.

'Take no heed of them, Mignonne. It weren't meant for you,' he told Bo kindly as she jumped onto his knee. 'It were just chance you were here. They didn' know. They pelt any fancy coach these days. They would set alight all things fine, they would. I hear tell they's been burning all the pretty windows, altars and crosses what they think wrong. But I don' set no store by them and their strict ways. No I do not. And I do say it is uncommon vile to call the queen such names, I do. French brat? Harlot? I never heard the like!'

Whilst the coach slowed and the pageboy marvelled at the splendour of St. James's Palace, Bo sat bolt upright on her seat, looked straight into the boy's grey eyes, and did her best to tell him that she liked him and wished him well.

Then she hopped down the steps and sat in the driveway.

There was a palace behind her, but she hardly noticed

it. Her sight was fixed on the coach as it turned to make its way home. Pieces of eggshell had stuck to its sides and there were scratches on its paintwork and splatters of rotten fruit on its horses.

She lay down on the warm cobbles and wondered why those people had thrown things, and why they'd called a queen such horrible names. She watched the coach disappear, then she yawned and put her head on her paws for a well-earned nap.

CHAPTER SEVEN
Bo's House.
The 21st Century

Bo's cellar was just as she'd left it. Nothing had changed. The spaniel was still sitting in the bright, still light of the coal hole, and Bo's paw was still resting on his back.

She lowered her leg.

'Can you dream about things you've never seen?' she asked.

'I wouldn't have thought so,' the spaniel replied.

'Me neither,' said Bo. 'Rabbits, squirrels, frogs - I can dream those. I know what they look like. But potage and coaches and portrait painters? I couldn't make them up if I tried.'

The spaniel bowed.

'Then you have learnt the first three lessons,' he said. 'Listen, trust, and believe. And now I can tell you something.'

He paused.

'You saw a spaniel being fed with venison broth, and I told you that spaniel was me.'

'Did you?'

'Yes. This was before you'd learnt to listen. What I

didn't tell you is that the chap who was doing the feeding, the man who was sitting opposite you at the table, was my master, King Charles the First of England, Scotland and Ireland.'

Bo gasped and took a step back.

'My name is Cavendish,' the spaniel said, 'and I was the king's most favoured pet and canine companion.'

Bo bowed low.

'No need for that,' said Cavendish. 'You were Mignonne, remember. You were Her Majesty The Queen's much-loved poodle.'

'*The Queen*?' Bo gasped. 'That lady was a *queen*?'

'My master's wife,' Cavendish nodded. 'You belonged to my master's wife, Queen Henrietta Maria.'

Bo folded her paws over her head.

'Oh, no,' she groaned.

'I can't understand why you didn't realise that,' Cavendish chuckled. 'Her Majesty took you to Mr Van Dyck's studio, did she not?'

'Yes, she did. I was having my portrait painted.'

'And did no one call her Your Majesty? Did they not bow when she entered the room?'

'Yes,' Bo replied. 'All of that. But, well, I don't know. I didn't realise that meant she was a queen. It just didn't occur to me. Oh, Cavendish, I behaved so badly! I ran out of the studio and a boy had to catch me!'

'It was Mignonne who ran, not you,' said Cavendish gently. 'Had you been thinking her thoughts rather than yours, we might know why she did it. Now we never will. It was unlike her. She loved being the centre of attention. Perhaps she was unwell that day, or just in a difficult mood.'

'I could do it again,' suggested Bo. 'I could be good next time. Mignonne could be good.'

'No. Lesson four. What's done is done and in the past. History can be repeated, but it can never be changed.'

'And what about you?' asked Bo. 'If you were King Charles's dog, how did you end up here, in *my* house?'

Cavendish took a deep breath.

'Well,' he began, 'when I died, I was sent away to be stuffed.'

'*Stuffed?*'

'Yes. Taxidermy was the new fashion, and still slightly experimental at the time. I was an early example, and not a terribly successful one, as you witnessed. They didn't have preservatives then, so being stuffed involved a lot of tugging and a great deal of straw. By the time they'd finished with me, only the eyes were anything like the original, and they were made of glass. It was a humiliating experience. Perhaps it's a good thing that my master never saw me again...'

Cavendish swallowed.

'...the king's circumstances changed, you see,' he continued. 'He wasn't able to collect me, and when the taxidermist closed his studio, I was sold off. I had a fancy glass cabinet in those days, but it broke, somewhere along the line. I can't remember how I ended up here. I do remember thinking it was probably the place, that you'd come here eventually.'

'You mean you've been waiting for me?' Bo asked

incredulously.

'Of course,' said Cavendish. 'We share more than our past, Bo. We share a rare gift, a gift of extraordinary power, but it cannot be harnessed unless we are together. Without you, I was nothing but a husk. Without me, you were just an ordinary dog. Together, though, we are invincible. Time holds no barriers for us. We can spend the present as we like and you'll miss barely a second of your life upstairs. As for the past, you can revisit it as often and for as long as you please.'

'I'm not sure I want to,' said Bo. 'At least not until I know more about how this works.'

'And you will,' Cavendish replied. 'You're learning something new and, just like anything else, it'll get easier with practice. You'll always have me to help you. I'll always make sure you get home again, but you'll find things a lot easier if you stop trying to be Bo and just go with the flow. You'll gain a lot more confidence, that way.'

'Go with the flow?'

'Go with the flow, Bo. Enjoy being Mignonne. See the world through her eyes. Think her thoughts. Live the life you once lived. Live Mignonne's life.'

'Did you know her well?' Bo asked.

'Very well indeed. You could say we were best friends. We went through a lot together.'

'What was she like?'

'Very pretty. She was more petite than you but she wasn't skinny.'

'I meant what was she *like*, she comes across as very

41

spoilt.'

'Terribly spoilt,' Cavendish chuckled. 'She could be a real brat. But she changed. She was a tough little thing, really.'

'And the queen?'

'You've met the queen.'

'Yes, but I didn't realise who she was. I thought she was just a lady.'

'Then we must try to find a day when Mignonne saw more of her,' said Cavendish. 'Let me think now...ah, yes! Do you like the seaside?'

'I don't know. I've never been there.'

'That's good,' Cavendish replied. 'It'll be easier to be Mignonne if you have no preconceptions. But now you really *should* go to bed.'

'I thought I was going to the seaside.'

'Another time,' said Cavendish. 'You can go to the seaside another time.'

Bo made many visits to Cavendish over the next few days and nights. She and the spaniel became firm friends, and since time was on hold when they were together, Bo never lost more than a few seconds of her normal life.

She learned to listen, to trust, and to believe what Cavendish told her. She began to have faith in the mysterious spaniel, and was flattered and pleased when he finally announced that the time had come for her to visit the seaside, where she must try not to have Bo thoughts, but go with the flow, and be Mignonne through and through.

CHAPTER EIGHT
The Port of Dover, England.
23rd February 1642

Mignonne glanced over her shoulder to check that King Charles and Queen Henrietta Maria were still amongst the huddle of people at the foot of the cliffs. When she saw they hadn't moved, she trotted happily along the wooden jetty and sat down in its centre to wait. Gulls wheeled around her and searched for scraps of fish from the morning catch, but she ignored them. She was too intent on her own game.

When a swell of water rushed towards her, crashed against the jetty's side with a slap and sprayed her with its freezing, salty mist, she leapt up and barked at it. Then she did a little prancing jig and, trembling with cold and expectation, sat down to wait for the next wave.

The first time she'd seen the sea, just two days previously, she'd hated it. She hadn't liked its smell, its noise, or even its colour, and no one, not even the queen, had been able to persuade her off the safe, grassy banks and onto the uneven stones and squidgy sand that led down to its edge.

By the second day, though, Mignonne had got bored of sitting on her own in the inn, and had ventured out behind King Charles when he took his early morning walk.

She'd hung back when he'd headed for the shoreline. She'd sat on the grass and watched from a safe distance as the sea rumbled and charged towards him on a thousand white horses. It had taken her a while, but eventually she'd realised that the water never came higher than a certain point, and that its attacks weren't aimed at the king personally. It was then that she'd stepped onto the stones and wobbled towards him.

The closer she'd got to her master, the easier it had become. The stones had turned to pebbles and softly rounded grit, and when she'd found she was running over soft, damp sand, the king had laughed and stamped his foot to splash them both. Suddenly, her fear had gone, and even when the water had sucked at her feet and dragged the grit and pebbles out from under them, she'd barked with joy.

Mignonne loved the sea now, but she didn't want to get *into* it or even *onto* it. Not even on a ship.

She stood up, shook herself and looked across the harbour. The dock was almost clear of the crates, boxes and trunks which had been stacked along it earlier that morning. They'd gradually been loaded aboard and were now either on the ship they called The Lion, or on one of the baggage vessels berthed either side of her. Only a few forlorn pieces were still waiting at the foot of the gangplanks, where a small crowd had gathered excitedly. They'd come to witness a happy royal occasion. The queen's eldest daughter, Princess Mary, had just got married, and now she and her mother were about to sail to Holland to settle Mary into her new home.

But the trip had another, more important and much more sinister purpose, about which the crowd had no idea.

The queen was fleeing for her life.

Mignonne recalled Van Dyck's warning about a brewing storm, and the way the eggs had been thrown at his coach. At the time, she hadn't made the link. She'd thought the egg-throwing was a one-off occurrence, but she was soon proved wrong. She'd seen lots of angry people since that day. She didn't know exactly what they were so upset about, but it was something to do with the king and queen. She'd overheard their conversations and seen them become ever more nervous and afraid. Now the king had persuaded his wife to leave the country, at least for the moment.

The ships' crews were sluicing the decks with water or tinkering with ropes and rigging, and on The Lion herself, a small boy had shinned up the main mast and was now straddled over a pole and shuffling along on his bottom. True, his skinny feet were braced against a safety rope, but he was a long, long way above the deck and having to stretch to tug the sails straight.

Mignonne shivered and turned away.

She didn't want to see the boy fall, and anyway she

was cold and wet. She heard the queen calling for her, and scampered over to the royal party, stood on her hind legs and scrabbled at her mistress's silk skirts with her wet paws.

The queen laughed nervously.

'Mignonne likes the sea,' she said. 'It is a good sign, non?'

Her voice was shaking.

'A very good sign, my love,' the king replied. 'But you should not worry so. Never was an English queen lost at sea, my sweet. The crossing is short, the weather is fine. Fifteen hours under the good care of Admiral Mennes here, and you will be safely in Holland.'

He turned to the handsome man at his side.

'Is that not so, Sir John?'

Admiral Mennes bowed.

'His Majesty's ship The Lion,' he replied, proudly indicating his craft with an outstretched arm, 'has two decks and more than sixty guns! Her Majesty the Queen will be very safe.'

'Of course she will!' the king declared.

He squeezed the queen's hand in his and drew her sideways.

'Mennes is a good man and a valiant sailor,' he whispered urgently. 'It is for your own safety that you go. Would I not rather keep you here? Would I send you abroad and far away had I the choice? What are you afraid of? The sea? 'Tis the shortest possible distance. Think of the poor souls who sail for weeks to The Indies!'

The queen giggled.

'That's better,' said the king gently. 'Come, let's sit together in the coach for a few minutes. Shall we take Mignonne too?'

'Yes, yes,' said the queen.

Inside the coach, the king laid a blanket across his wife's lap, placed Mignonne on top of it and sat down.

'You cannot stay here,' he said as he put an arm around Henrietta Maria's shoulders. 'There are those who would put you to death.'

'I am more afraid of those who would put *you* to death,' the queen replied. 'I am afraid for *you*. You must stay firm with these people. Do not hesitate, Charles. If I hear that you have done so I shall be mad with fury. I will retire to a nunnery!'

She delved into the folds of her skirt and produced a silk pocket.

'You must write every day,' she said. 'I have made you a cipher. Be sure to say nothing important in your letters without using this code.'

Her fingers fumbled with the pocket's ties.

'My hands shake so,' she muttered.

The king reached out and took the pocket, untied it and removed a tightly rolled sheet of paper. He unravelled the mysterious scroll and Mignonne stepped onto his knee and peered at it.

On its left-hand side, neatly written in a column and listed in order, was the alphabet. Next to each letter was a one or two digit number. Each number was unique and random, with no obvious relationship to the letter beside it. The king examined this cipher, then returned it to the pocket, which he slipped into his sleeve.

'Take care it is not stolen,' the queen urged.

'I shall commit it to memory,' the king promised, 'then burn it. Meantime, all is aboard. I saw to that in person. Admiral Mennes has locked King Henry's gold collars in his cabin, and you have the Grand Sancy and the Mirror of Portugal.'

The queen frowned.

'Monsieur?'

Her husband looked alarmed and slapped a hand to his forehead.

'Don't tell me...' he began.

But then he caught sight of the mischievous glint in his wife's eyes.

He laughed, and she giggled back and slipped two fingers down the front of her bodice.

'The Grand Sancy,' she said.

She withdrew a diamond the size of a fat grape and allowed it to roll in the palm of her hand.

Mignonne sat up straight and stared at the jewel.

'It is pretty, non?' the queen teased.

She picked the stone up between her thumb and forefinger and held it against Mignonne's damp fur.

'Perhaps I may change my mind,' she said, 'and have it set instead. It would make a charming bauble for Mignonne, would it not?'

Mignonne wagged her tail and tried to pick the diamond up in her teeth.

'No,' said the king. 'The biggest diamond in Europe

is not meant for a dog, not even this dog.'

'Then we could use the Mirror of Portugal instead?' jested the queen as she produced a second stunning diamond.

Mignonne tipped her head and looked hopeful.

'Alas, Mignonne it is not to be,' the queen sighed.

'That stone,' the king said ruefully, 'once belonged to our great Queen Elizabeth. Now it will go to Holland and be sold to save the very throne on which she sat. We must have money to buy arms, Mignonne. We may need muskets and munitions one day soon, and these diamonds will pay for them.'

Henrietta Maria slipped the diamonds back into their hiding place and sighed.

'Queen Elizabeth will understand,' she said as she lifted Mignonne into her arms. 'Now Monsieur, let us put this boat of yours to the test.'

As The Lion and her baggage ships were towed out of the harbour and into open water, the crowd began to disperse, and the king asked for his horse. When it was brought to him, he took its reins and told the groom to return Mignonne to the coach.

'Be sure to wrap her up well,' he added. 'For she is shivering, and the queen will not forgive me should she catch a chill. Go quickly, now, and leave me be.'

With that he swung into the saddle, turned his horse's head towards the cliffs, and galloped away.

Back in the coach, Mignonne shook off her blanket and

slipped her head under the window blind nearest the sea. The Lion was cutting through the steel-grey waves with her cream-coloured sails stretched taut against the wind.

'Godspeed, mistress,' Mignonne muttered. 'Godspeed.'

She crossed to the other side of the coach and leant through its window.

At first she couldn't see the king, but then she spotted him, high up on top of the cliffs. He had halted his horse and taken off his hat. Now he was standing up in his stirrups, gazing out to sea and waving the hat in a sweeping arc.

Circling above him was a raven, a raven as black as the king's hat.

CHAPTER NINE
Bo's House.
The 21st Century

When Bo arrived home, she told Cavendish everything she could remember about her visit to Dover.

'And you never once had a Bo thought?'

'Not once. I was Mignonne from start to finish,' Bo replied proudly.

'Then you have learnt lesson five,' said Cavendish. 'Always be Mignonne when you're there. It makes things so much easier.'

'I can see that, now,' Bo agreed. 'Did things get easier for the king and queen, too? I hope so. Why did they have to sell diamonds for muskets?'

'In case things *didn't* get easier. They had to prepare themselves for the worst.'

'The brewing storm?'

Cavendish hesitated.

'Yes. But, you know, even storm clouds can have silver linings. The queen's trip to Holland was really the start of our friendship.'

'Because the king was looking after Mignonne?'

'Exactly. He hardly let her out of his sight, at least not

'til Prince Rupert came back.'

'Prince Rupert?' Bo sat up sharply. 'I saw his portrait at Mr Van Dyck's studio. Van Dyck said Rupert was brave and beautiful, that he was abroad, but that he might return one day and...oh!'

'What is it, Bo?'

'He...well, he also said that might not be a good sign.'

'He was right,' Cavendish replied. 'It wasn't. The storm was no longer "brewing", it was beginning to bubble over. Rupert came back to England to take charge of The King's Horse.'

Bo wrinkled her nose.

'That's odd,' she said. 'Because the king seemed very happy with his horse. He rode it onto the cliffs at Dover with no trouble at all, even when a raven flew round it.'

'A raven, you say? Mmm,' Cavendish muttered. 'I hadn't known about that. It may be the earliest recorded sighting...'

''Scuse me?' Bo asked.

'Nothing,' Cavendish replied. 'It's nothing at all. Now, where were we?'

'The king's horse?'

'Oh, yes. But I wasn't talking about the king's horse, singular. I meant the king's cavalry. That's thousands of horses, and when the real fighting between the king and his enemies began, Rupert was their commander. Mignonne was right there with him at the first battle.'

He looked sideways at Bo.

'You should try it,' he said.

'A battle?'

Cavendish nodded.

'I might be killed,' murmured Bo.

'Not you.'

'Mignonne?'

'Oh please,' said Cavendish. 'Do you think I'd send you to Mignonne's death? She loved riding, and she loved Rupert, and *you're* forgetting lesson five.'

"Be Mignonne when you're there," Bo recited.

She batted her ears with a paw.

'You won't forget about me?'

'No,' Cavendish promised. 'I won't forget about you. Not ever.'

'Then I'll go,' said Bo bravely.

'Good girl. Just remember to be Mignonne, and only Mignonne. And remember, too, that whatever happens, it happens to *her*, not to Bo. Ready? Close your eyes, now.'

Bo held up a paw.

'Stop!' she barked. 'I'm not sure. I think I'd really rather...'

But before she could finish her sentence, her eyes had closed of their own accord.

CHAPTER TEN
Edgehill, Oxfordshire, England.
23rd October 1642

Mignonne was asleep in the king's tent when Prince Rupert arrived, but the sound of her hero's footsteps made her drag her eyes open.

The king's guards drew back the tent flap, and the prince stepped through the opening.

Gone was the pale, boyish face which Bo had seen in the portrait at the studio. Rupert's features were now dark and chiselled, and his once golden curls were long and black and tied back with a scarlet ribbon. He had grown into a beautiful young man, just as Mr Van Dyck had described.

He strode towards Mignonne, scooped her up in his arms and kissed her, just as the king emerged, half-dressed, from behind a screen.

'Your Majesty,' Rupert bowed.

'Nephew,' the king responded. 'All ready?'

'Aye, Sire,' said Rupert hesitantly. 'All ready.'

'Then what?' asked the king, though he suspected he already knew the answer.

The first battle against his enemies, the

Parliamentarians, was imminent and, as Commander of The King's Horse, brilliant but impetuous Rupert should have been busy preparing the Royalist cavalry. Yet here he was, cuddling the queen's poodle like a lovesick girl.

'I hear tell that Boy is unwell,' the king prompted with a wry smile.

Mignonne pricked her ears. She knew all about Boy. Everyone did. He was a poodle, too, and was famous for being Rupert's adored pet and mascot. There were plenty of rude jokes about the glamorous prince, the battle-hardened dog and how they shared a bed, but they'd fought together in Europe, and Rupert was very superstitious about Boy's supposed powers. Mignonne had never met Boy, but Cavendish had. He'd described him as a nice enough but fairly ordinary dog, and not at all as special as Rupert liked to think. Even so, Boy's absence was clearly affecting the prince.

'He is most unwell,' he replied. 'He is in the care of a woman at the village of Radway.'

'As is Cavendish,' said the king.

'The woman is feeding him hourly with light chicken broth,' Rupert added.

'You mean Boy?' the king asked. 'Boy is being fed with light chicken broth.'

'Exactly so,' said Prince Rupert.

'Good,' the king laughed. 'Because were Cavendish to be fed with anything either light or chicken, I'd be hard-pressed to vouch for ankles.'

Rupert ran his hands through his hair.

'He does not have the heart for battle this day,' he

sighed.

'No?' the king goaded, 'and what of you? Do you have the heart for battle?'

Rupert hesitated.

'Not without Boy, eh? Oh, for heaven's sake Rupert. Come to the point, man. Your own poodle is sick and you want loan of the queen's. You want to take Mignonne for your mascot.'

Mignonne wriggled.

'Admit it, nephew, for I have neither time nor patience for this crab-like talk. You may take Mignonne. She rides well enough, but she may stay aboard only until the start. After that she will be collected by your groom and taken to the safety of your tent, where she will remain for the duration. You know that Her Majesty the Queen would never forgive me if anything happened her?'

Prince Rupert nodded.

'Then enough said. Now go prepare your troops. I'll see you at the inspection.'

Less than an hour later, Mignonne was lying across the pommel of Prince Rupert's saddle. She had one paw on the reins and the other draped nonchalantly over her horse's shoulder. Immediately next to her, riding a magnificent white horse, was the king. He was wearing a sublime black velvet cloak and dinky matching cap, both lined with ermine, and was surrounded by Royalist officers and standard-bearers in bright silk coats, coloured sashes and steel body armour. Some carried guns on the front of their saddles, and all had handsome swords which glinted against their horses' sides, whilst the huge curly feathers in their hats, and the flags above their heads, fluttered in the breeze. Mignonne was sporting an ice-blue leather collar and a rather fetching little sash with a silver fringe.

She pressed her cheek against her horse's withers and sniffed. She loved its smell of warmth and straw, leather and wax. She liked the sounds it made too, the creak of its saddle, its snorts, and the way it stamped its feet.

She shuffled sideways and tugged on its reins with her teeth, just so she could hear the chink of its bit. It turned to look at her with one round, brown eye, and puckered its lips.

'Owp!' she yelped, though the horse's soft muzzle had come nowhere near her.

'Enough of that, you two,' Rupert laughed. 'Look, Mignonne. Here are the boys!'

Two gleaming ponies trotted alongside Mignonne, and she raised her head and barked hello to the king's sons. Prince Charles was now twelve, and his little brother James was nine. They were both wearing miniature body armour and looked excited, though Mignonne could see they were trembling too, and that behind their fixed smiles their teeth were chattering.

She gave them an encouraging yap and they raised their hands and waved at her.

'Mignonne! Mignonne!' they called, rather shakily.

When the king had inspected his troops and given some last words of encouragement, his commanders issued

their final orders and everyone dispersed to their battle stations.

Rupert and Mignonne rode out to the cavalry and took their place at its head. It was standing on top of a slope, and since Mignonne was in the front row, she had a clear view of everything.

A mile across the valley, thousands of Parliamentarians, or 'Roundheads' as they were nowadays known, were shuffling into position and forming orderly blocks. From where Mignonne was sitting, they looked like pieces in a giant board game. Mignonne knew that it wasn't strictly correct to call them 'Roundheads'. That was a nickname for devout Puritans, who cut their hair in a pudding-basin style. It didn't apply to every Parliamentarian. Many of them weren't Puritan at all, but the name had stuck. They were all 'Roundheads' now.

Mignonne glanced to her left.

Beyond the cavalry were the Royalist musketeers and dragoons, and several massive, hedgehog-shapes. Cavendish had told her all about these hedgehogs. Every one of their quills was a spiked pole, and each pole was carried by a man.

The men were called pikemen, and their job was to stand firm against oncoming cavalry. No horse could be made to gallop into what appeared to be a solid wall. It would swerve, and a thousand swerving horses would cause absolute havoc.

Mignonne shuddered at the thought.

Yet the pikemen's success depended on every man holding his ground. If just one of them lost his nerve and ran, the whole company would break up, and the horses would gallop straight over them, into the heart of the enemy.

Mignonne shuddered again and struggled upright in her saddle as a drummer appeared and marched, head held high, across the Royalist front line. She gazed at the man's fluttering wrists as he beat the drumsticks against the snare, then passed in front of her, looked her straight in the eye, and played her a special roll.

Bbrruh-bbrrruh, bbriimm-bbriimm!
Bbrruh-bbrrruh, bbriimm-bbriimm!

The drumbeats had sent a ripple of excitement through the cavalry, and now the horses were fighting their bits, rolling their eyes and pawing at the ground. Harnesses chinked, officers called to each other across the ranks, and flags and standards made snapping noises in the wind. The battle was about to begin.

CHAPTER ELEVEN

The opening shots were fired by Parliamentarian cannon, and shortly after that the king himself lit the first Royalist gun. The odd cannonball whizzed across the fields, and the air was filled with puffs of acrid smoke, but the cannons themselves took so long to load that minutes passed between volleys.

It was a very slow start. Even the horses got bored. They were desperate to charge, and started plunging about and whinnying. Rupert's own mount was jogging on the spot and tossing his head so violently that his mane and the foam from his mouth kept splatting Mignonne in the face.

She began to wish she was somewhere else and tried to remember what the king had said. Wasn't she supposed to be taken to Rupert's tent?

She wriggled.

'Hold still there!' Rupert shouted in her ear.

He lifted his weight off the saddle and slid a leather bag out from underneath him. It was the size of a small pillowcase and was buckled to the saddle with tough leather straps.

'You shall be my mascot for the first charge,

Mignonne,' he called over the din. 'Fear it not.'

Mignonne glanced at him anxiously.

He seemed incredibly calm.

He reached behind his head and removed the scarlet ribbon from his hair.

'Do you see the sprigs of leaves my men are wearing?' he asked.

Mignonne looked about.

Sure enough, everybody seemed to have a small bunch of foliage tucked into their hats or pinned to their shoulders.

'They are field-signs,' Rupert explained. 'So they can be recognised. This will be yours.'

He tied the scarlet ribbon around Mignonne's neck.

'There,' he said. 'Now everyone will know you are the Mascot of the General of Horse.'

He slipped an arm under Mignonne's chest and lowered her, tail first, into the leather bag, then swung the bag sideways and rested it against his horse's shoulder.

'Give me good fortune and victory this day, little Mignonne,' he said as he ruffled the top of her head. 'Hold on tight, now!' he added.

He stood up in his stirrups, drew his sword, and raised it in the air whilst Mignonne manoeuvred herself into a more comfortable position and poked her nose over the top of the bag.

'Don't jump!' Rupert called down to her. 'Whatever you do, don't jump! You'll be trampled to death!'

Mignonne thought he was probably right about that. Her horse and the others around it seemed vaguely out of control. Their heads were high in the air, well above their bits, and they were lifting their front legs off the ground and leaning back on their hocks in a rocking motion.

Mignonne was rocking with them when a trumpet sounded.

High above her head, Rupert waved his sword from side to side, then sat down in the saddle with a thump. His horse and all the others around it leapt into a trot, and Mignonne's heart leapt into her mouth.

The horses were packed really close together, now. Rupert's stirrups were clashing with those either side of him. Men were calling to each other and having to shout to make themselves heard. The noise was terrific, but it was condensed and controlled, just like the steady rhythm of the trotting hooves.

O*ne*-two, *one*-two, *one*-two.

'Hold fast!' Rupert roared.

O*ne*-two, *one*-two, *one*-two.

'Holding trot!' someone roared back.

Mignonne's teeth knocked together as she bounced against her horse's shoulder.

'Canter!' screamed Rupert.

'Canter!' came the reply.

One-two-three, *one*-two-three.

'CHAAARGE!'

Rupert's horse squealed and kicked out.

'CHAAARGE!'

Clods of earth flew up, a thousand swords were whisked from their scabbards, and Mignonne looked down.

The ground was a blur of pounding hooves.

She pressed her hind feet hard against the base of her leather pouch, straightened up, and stared past her horse's undulating neck.

Each stride brought her closer to the Roundhead army.

She could see their pikemen now.

The tips of their hedgehog quills seemed to be pointing straight at her. Her horse had seen them too, and was lowering its head, ears pricked, to get a better view.

Mignonne swallowed and closed her eyes. Which was best? That the horse should swerve and bring its thousand or so companions crashing down around it? Or that the pikemen should break ranks and let the horses charge over them?

She felt her horse's shoulder rise beneath her and knew that it was turning. She heard cries and whinnies and pistol shots but nothing crashed into her, and, rather than galloping on, the horse began to slow.

Mignonne's eyes snapped open.

'They are fleeing the field!' Rupert cried.

Sure enough, a wing of enemy cavalry had peeled away and was hurtling into the distance.

'Hold fast!' Rupert cried again. 'Hold, I say! Leave them be! Oh, pox,' he added under his breath, 'my men are giving chase, Mignonne!'

He leant out of his saddle and grabbed the reins of the nearest Royalist horseman.

'Here,' he shouted to the startled man, a sergeant. 'Take this little dog to my groom.'

He manhandled Mignonne out of her leather bag and over the gap between him and the sergeant.

'Tell him to put her in my tent. And mind how you go, for she belongs to the queen, and heads will roll if she is not safe and well at the end of this day.'

Then he galloped away to catch up with his men.

The sergeant, who would far rather have been chasing Roundhead troopers than delivering a poodle, made it to Rupert's groom in record time. The groom then took Mignonne to Prince Rupert's tent, set her down beside a bowl of water, and left.

Mignonne stood in the middle of the floor and listened to the beat of drums, the blast of cannons, the crack of muskets and the screams of men and horses. Then she scrabbled into a corner and buried her head under a cushion. She folded her paws across it, pressed it hard against her ears to muffle the noise, and fell fast asleep.

She awoke an hour or so later to find that the light and the battle sounds had faded. She stood up, yawned and stretched, and pushed the tent flap open with her nose. Outside, there was no one around and, as she pottered about sniffing for rabbits and squirrels, she was soon lost in a doggy world of smells and possibilities.

She had a buck rabbit in her sights when she heard the

snort of a horse. She took no notice until she realised that the horse, and several others, were coming her way. Then she jolted to her senses and remembered the battle.

She left the path she was on and darted behind a bush for safety. From there she watched the horsemen approach. They were shrouded in mist, hardly more than silhouettes against the darkening sky. Only when they drew level with her could she tell that they were far better armed than the Royalists she'd seen. They were bristling with weapons, but also wearing very simple, rather stark-looking clothes.

They were Roundheads.

She shrank deeper into the shelter of the bush and held her breath whilst the men trotted past, apparently aimlessly.

When they'd gone, she came out from her hiding place and realised she'd travelled far further than she'd intended.

She was lost.

She raised her nose, but the air was too full of acrid smoke for her to detect anything useful in the way of scent. She tipped her head and listened for something which might give her a bearing, but the battle noises, though much fainter now, were scattered all around her. She heard a distant shot and whipped round, but then another rang out from the opposite direction. Far away to her right, someone shouted, and then there was another shout, and a whinny to her left.

She was dizzy by now.

She heard more horses, nearby and coming closer.

She heard people talking and recognised the voices of the king's sons, Prince Charles and Prince James.

She sighed with relief and slumped onto the path to wait for them. Then she heard the jangle of swords and stirrups and realised that the Roundhead troopers were returning.

She barked.

Someone in the princes' party said something about 'a dog'.

She barked again, and heard Prince James's voice behind her.

'That sounds like Mignonne,' he said.

'It can't be,' Prince Charles replied. 'Papa said she must stay in Rupert's tent.'

The troopers were close now, and heading straight for the princes. Mignonne could see both parties so clearly that she couldn't believe they hadn't spotted one another. When at last they did, they seemed to think they were meeting up with friends from their own side, and kept on riding. The gap between them had narrowed to a few lengths and Mignonne was growing frantic when Prince Charles suddenly realised what was happening.

'I fear them not!' he cried, drawing his pistol.

One of the Roundheads then recognised the prince and shouted for his friends to help capture the king's son. He spurred his horse and it bounded forward, but then caught sight of Mignonne sitting on the path, and swerved away in fright.

This gave Mignonne an idea and she charged up the path, straight at the troopers' horses, who didn't hear her paws on the soft ground until it was too late. When they finally spotted a black missile hurtling towards them at knee-height, they shied spectacularly.

They twisted and reared in the air, and Mignonne, who was well aware of the dangers of hooves, shot sideways to avoid having them crash down on her. As she did so, something caught hold of her and wrenched her backwards. She was flung in the air and dropped. She hit the ground with a thud, bounced, and saw a falling trooper fly past. She felt the warm underbelly of a horse brush against her fur, and then she dropped again, not right to the ground this time, but to just inches above it. For a moment she swung there, but then there was a leap and a whoosh, and she was on the move again. Ruts and holes, stones, fallen twigs and tufts of grass sped along beneath her, and by the time the bolting horse came to a stop, she was barely conscious.

The horse pawed the ground and shook itself violently. Mignonne's sash snapped on the girth buckle which had snagged it, and she slipped to the ground as the horse wandered off without her.

CHAPTER TWELVE

When she opened her eyes, night had fallen, and she was lying in a landscape of jagged edges and soft mounds.

A horse was stretched out beside her in the moonlight. It appeared to be dead, mouth open, tongue lolling to one side. She shifted her weight and raised her throbbing head. Someone groaned nearby. She struggled into a sitting position and began to make things out.

The jagged edges were splintered gun carriages, discarded pikes and charred trees. The mounds were bodies. The moon was shining on horses and lighting up the faces of men. She could see hands, bare shoulders and chests, white feathers and glinting swords.

She stood up, and the frost in her fur crackled and sprayed around her.

She stepped over the muzzle of the dead horse and limped towards the groaning sound. She passed a drummer and glanced down, then swiftly back up again. She hoped it wasn't *her* drummer but she couldn't bear to take a second look, and anyway there was nothing she could do for the man.

Several paces further on, she heard the groan again. This time it was right beside her and, as she leant over the boy, it wasn't the way his left arm had been torn away from below the elbow that caught her attention, but rather his eyes.

They were open, staring up at the stars, and their pale greyness was startling.

She bent to nuzzle the boy's remaining hand.

It was stone cold.

She lay down, rested her head on his chest, and was surprised and relieved to feel some warmth and a faint heartbeat. She barked, and the boy's eyes flickered. She barked again, and he tilted his head towards her.

''Tis Mignonne,' he muttered. ''Tis Mignonne I do say, an' therefore I knows I am gone to heaven, praise be.'

The boy rolled onto his side, taking Mignonne with him and flinging his good arm over her body. Even so, she was cold. Really cold. Her paws were so frozen she could no longer feel them. She knew she should wriggle out from under the boy and try to keep moving, but all she wanted to do was sleep.

When she heard her name being called, she twitched and growled in what she believed to be a dream.

'Mignonne!' the voice repeated. 'Gad, where are you? Please God she is alive,' it muttered despairingly, 'their Majesties will never forgive me. *I* will never forgive me.'

Still believing she was asleep, Mignonne whimpered, but as she did so she saw a horse's hoof, a living, walking, horse's hoof. She whimpered again, and the response that came was clear and real and the best, most welcome sound she'd ever heard.

'Mignonne?' Prince Rupert whispered. 'Is that you? Have I found you at last?'

He leapt from his horse with a soft thud and Mignonne wagged her tail as he knelt down beside her on the frosty ground, reached out a hand, and stroked her.

'You're so cold!' he whispered.

He removed his cloak and prized her out from under the injured boy, then wrapped her up warmly and held her close to his chest.

'This boy might have kept you warm a while,' he said, 'but not lately.'

Mignonne wriggled in Rupert's arms.

'Parliamentarian,' he added. 'So young he is to die like this.'

Mignonne pawed at his hand.

'Yes, yes. We'll go now,' he said. 'We will warm you up and find you something to eat, though heaven knows where.'

'No, you don't understand,' thought Mignonne. 'I can't leave the boy. He is still alive, and he was so kind to me that day at the studio.'

When Rupert moved to stand, Mignonne struggled free from his grasp and shook off the cloak, but she was weaker than she'd realised. The effort sapped her strength and she fell clumsily against the boy's injured arm.

There was a quick gasp of pain.

'Oh no! Poor you,' Mignonne barked, 'I'm so sorry.'

'Blessed be!' Rupert exclaimed.

He bent his head and laid it gently on the boy's chest.

'There is a faint beat!' he said.

'Stretcher!' he called, waving his cloak in the air. 'Over here!'

Then he scraped his hair off his forehead and seemed to have second thoughts.

'No. There is a quicker way. I shall take him myself. I will make straight for Mr Harvey. If anyone can save the lad, it's him.'

He draped his cloak over the boy and lifted him gently off the ground. Then he reached for his horse and placed the boy over the front of its saddle. Finally, he picked Mignonne up and, holding her firmly in the crook of his arm, remounted.

'We must go slowly,' he muttered. 'This is difficult ground at best, and it will be a hard task to balance a boy and a dog on a stumbling horse.'

Prince Rupert rode in silence with one hand steadying the boy and the other wrapped tightly around Mignonne. He held the reins by their buckle and let the horse stretch its neck and pick its way over the many discarded weapons and injured or dead men. Hoarfrost twinkled on the ground and in the surrounding hedges and, when Rupert spoke at last, his warm breath came out in clouds.

'I reckon to a thousand slain,' he said. 'Perhaps twice that many are wounded.'

He paused.

'You saw how it began, Mignonne,' he added. 'Both

sides holding fire 'til the other was ready? Such decorum! That is soon forgotten. The cavalry make their charge, and men are scattered. Soon they are fighting hand-to-hand. Sword, pike, matchlock. 'Tis always a messy business, and so devilish that dead men stand upright in the crush. Both sides will celebrate a victory tonight, yet neither can truly claim one. We followed the Roundhead cavalry, you know. That was our mistake. We should have let them go but...'

He gathered his reins and his horse whipped up its head, ears pricked.

'Stand aside!' Rupert shouted. 'Move away and be gone!'

Three shadowy figures scuttled past and disappeared into the gloom.

'Robbers,' Rupert spat. 'Come to take whatever they can find. Weapons, clothes, jewellery too, if they happen across a wealthy knight. They'll squabble over dead bodies and strip the injured down to the last shred. Lower than London rats, they are.'

When the strange little party reached the king's encampment, Rupert called for his groom. He removed the injured boy from his saddle and asked the groom to take the horse and Mignonne to the makeshift stables. There, braziers were burning and someone had managed to make a pot of rabbit stew. The groom wrapped Mignonne in a blanket, set her down near one of the fires, and brought her a ladleful of hot rabbit gravy.

She sipped it gratefully and fell into a fitful sleep.

Dawn broke, and she felt the touch of a hand on her back. She opened her eyes to find Prince Rupert leaning over her. Now she saw what she hadn't noticed the night before, when it was so dark and she was so cold. She saw for the first time how Rupert's silk sleeves and buff leather coat were splattered with damp soil and other men's blood. She looked up at his beautiful face and realised it was grey with tiredness, smoke and dust. He looked exhausted.

'Wake up, little Mignonne,' he said softly. 'Your soldier boy is asking for you. He's been calling you by name, though I cannot for the life of me think how he knows it. He is much improved.'

Mignonne stood up and shook herself.

'Mr Harvey says he will live,' Prince Rupert continued, 'and that his upper arm might yet be saved, all thanks to you. And the cold. Harvey has the whimsical notion that it was the cold that stopped him from bleeding to death. Let me take that now.'

Mignonne had forgotten all about Rupert's scarlet hair ribbon. Now he untied it from around her neck and slipped it into his sleeve.

The boy was lying at the far end of a dressing station.

His eyes were closed and what remained of his left arm was tightly bandaged. His right lay across his chest, its pale hand being held and gently stroked by Prince Charles.

'Mr Harvey said from the very first that he thought he knew the boy,' Prince Charles said quietly. 'Now he's realised why. When Sir Anthony Van Dyck was dying, Harvey visited him many a time. He remembers that this boy was the painter's page.'

'Then that is how he knows Mignonne!' Prince Rupert exclaimed.

'It must be. And now father says he should be given employ, even though he is Parliamentarian. In London it was easier to enlist for Parliament than it was to join the king, and anyway he might only have done it for the jape.'

'And some clothes and food, perhaps,' Rupert added. 'But he looks too young to enlist.'

Prince Charles nodded.

'Mr Harvey recalls he's always been a mite, and thinks he must be *near* enough sixteen. But look! He is opening his eyes. Lift Mignonne up now, Rupert. Let him see her.'

The strange grey eyes looked blank at first, but then there was a flicker of recognition, and the boy smiled.

'Mignonne,' he whispered. ''Tis Mignonne, I do say.'

'Leave him now,' Prince Rupert smiled. 'Let him sleep. You must rest too, Charles, for I hear tell that your first battle was a close run thing. You came across Roundhead troopers, did you not?'

'Yes!' Prince Charles replied. 'And I would have shot them all!'

'Aye,' Rupert laughed. 'No doubt you would, had it not been for some divine intervention.'

Charles nodded disappointedly.

'A trooper charged at us. He came within a whisker of my shooting him stone dead but something scared his horse. The others shied and scattered, too. One even threw its rider and bolted towards the battlefield.'

'A rabbit, perhaps?' Rupert suggested.

'I don't know. Something like that. But the strangest thing is that I swear I heard a dog bark. James thought it was Mignonne, but I told him it couldn't be her because papa had said she must stay in your tent.'

'And she did,' Rupert lied. 'At least until the battle was over. Then I took her out to the field myself. That's how we found the boy.'

'Then the dog must have been a local one,' said Charles, 'a stray, perhaps.'

Rupert nodded.

'There's no other explanation,' he said as he drew his cloak over Mignonne's damp and tangled fur.

CHAPTER THIRTEEN
Bo's House.
The 21st Century

'You see?' said Cavendish. 'I told you I wouldn't forget about you, and now you're safely home again. How was it? What did you make of it all?'

Bo replied as best she could, though it all came out in a rush.

'I thought I was just going to watch but then Rupert put me on his horse and we charged and then I went looking for rabbits and I saw Roundhead troopers and they wanted to capture Prince Charles so I frightened their horses and my sash got caught on one of the girths and the horse bolted and I woke up on the battlefield which was completely horrible but the good thing was that I found a wounded boy and he'd been Mr Van Dyck's page so I recognised him and Prince Rupert carried him to Mr Harvey and now they think the boy will live and the king might give him a job but Rupert said that nobody really won the battle.'

She gasped for breath.

'No,' Cavendish said quietly. 'Nobody really did. If they had, things might have stopped there and then. As it was, there were many more battles to come.'

'How many more?' Bo wheezed.

'Many, many more,' Cavendish replied.

'A war, then?'

'The English Civil War.'

'But why?' Bo wondered aloud. 'Why were they fighting? No. Don't tell me. I already know. Humans are always fighting. I've seen it on TV and it's always about the same three things.'

'Oh, yes?'

'Yes. Religion, money and power. That's what humans fight about. Though personally I think it all comes down to money.'

'That's very insightful, Bo,' said Cavendish.

He sighed and lay down.

'Looking back, I can see the mistakes my master made,' he said sadly. 'His reign had been a happy one until the troubles began.'

Bo could see that Cavendish was upset. It was hard for him to admit that his master hadn't been perfect.

'I think the king was quite shy,' she ventured.

'He was!' Cavendish exclaimed. 'I'm so glad you can see that about him. He was hopeless with strangers. People thought he was arrogant and haughty.'

'He wasn't really though,' Bo added, relieved to have said the right thing. 'He was kind and loving to his friends and family.'

She snuggled up to Cavendish and rested a paw on his shoulder.

'Tell me what happened,' she prompted. 'Tell me

where it all went wrong.'

'Thank you. Yes. I'll try.'

Cavendish took a deep breath.

'My master was very religious. He enjoyed his prayers and liked to worship in decorative surroundings. You know the sort of thing. Stained-glass windows, candles, gold chalices...'

'So? What's wrong with that?'

'Nothing. Except that austere religious groups hated all that stuff. Particularly the Puritans. They thought the king was trying to turn England into a Catholic country. He wasn't, but the row spread anyway and he soon realised he needed an army to keep the peace. That would cost...'

'Money,' interjected Bo.

Cavendish nodded.

'Money was something only a Parliament could grant, and the king had no Parliament. Like many kings, he believed that only God could tell him how to rule. Suddenly, though, he had no choice. He had to go cap in hand to the very people he'd been ignoring and they, of course, divided into supporters and detractors.'

'The Royalists and the Parliamentarians,' said Bo. 'You haven't mentioned the queen. How did she fit into all this?'

'Not well. She had no time for politics. Her brother was the king of France and reigned supreme, so she saw no reason why Charles couldn't do the same. She was also a Catholic, as the king's enemies kept pointing out. It all made her a sitting target for propaganda, and worse, and she must have been afraid, but she was also stubborn as a mule. She soon came back to England.'

CHAPTER FOURTEEN
The Deanery, Christ Church, Oxford, England.
January 1644

With England in the grip of war, the king and queen moved their court from London to the much safer town of Oxford.

The university buildings were turned into stores for grain and munitions, foundries for the manufacture of cannon, and tailors' shops for the making of military uniforms. The town's quadrangles were penned for cattle and horses, its mediaeval houses were packed with officers and courtiers, and its streets and taverns were brimful of soldiers. Food was short, the drains were blocked, and fires were constantly breaking out in the overcrowded wooden buildings. There was disease and squalor, and people held dirty socks to their noses or plugged their nostrils with bitter absinthe to disguise the stench in the streets. Yet for all that, life in Oxford was exciting and lively, even for the poor. They could gawp at swashbuckling Cavaliers propping up the tavern bars and watch glamorous ladies parade about in the latest continental fashions. There were plays to see, music and poetry to listen to, and gossipy parties for the rich to attend.

In London, where the Parliamentarians had taken control, the living conditions were just as bad, if not worse, but Puritan attitudes had also closed the theatres and banned all frivolities, including the roasting of dinners for Christmas.

The king's apartments at Oxford were in the Deanery at Christ Church, and His Majesty had a favourite room there, which he'd taken as his study. This was where his friends and military commanders came to visit him, where he wrote or dictated letters, and where he kept all his papers and books. Every available surface in this room was piled high with maps, treaties, battle plans and correspondence. Only the floor was clear of papers, and that was where Mignonne and Cavendish spent most of their days, especially when it was cold outside.

Mignonne couldn't lie as close to the fire as Cavendish did. Her dense black curls absorbed more heat than his glossy, partially white coat. So, whilst he curled up on the rug in front of the hearth, Mignonne would settle herself a short distance away, and lie on her back with her paws in the air.

On one particular morning, the king's study was even busier than usual, and with all the comings and goings, and the fire being kept constantly alight, the heat soon built up.

Then, quite suddenly, everyone left, and Cavendish and Mignonne found themselves alone in the stifling atmosphere.

'I think I may have to go elsewhere,' Cavendish said. 'This place is too hot, even for me.'

He barked, and the guards on the far side of the door shuffled their feet, but the door didn't open.

'Cats!' he swore. 'Why won't they let us out?'

'Because they're not allowed to,' said Mignonne patiently. 'They're *guards*. They're supposed to *guard* the king's things. Anyway, it's getting dark. His Majesty will be home soon.'

'What's the point of having guards who look after the king's things but leave his dogs to suffocate?' Cavendish growled.

His ears pricked. Someone was approaching the door.

'Quick, Mignonne,' he said, 'help me get their attention.'

The combination of Cavendish's deep bark and Mignonne's plaintive howl was too much to ignore, and soon the door opened partway, and a pair of familiar grey eyes poked through the gap.

The boy whom Rupert and Mignonne had rescued at Edgehill was back in his old job as a page, this time to the two princes, Charles and James.

His name was Richard Cheevely, and he was very proud of his new post and the smart uniform that came with it. He often reminded Mignonne how clever she'd been to find him on the battlefield and almost certainly save his life. His upper arm had been saved too, but it still ached sometimes, and though he never complained,

Mignonne occasionally saw him flinch with pain.

'My, 'tis warm in here,' Cheevely told the guards. 'That's why they's be barkin'. They's be wantin' out an' cool off.'

'Can't let 'em out,' came the curt reply. 'Can't let nothin' in or out. That's what we've been told.'

'Then I could open the window, perhaps,' Cheevely suggested.

'Buck up then,' Cavendish groaned.

'Don' know 'bout that,' said the guard.

'You could watch me,' Cheevely continued. 'There can't be no wrong in that. If His Majesty should complain, which I don't see that he would, then I shall say that Cavendish and little Mignonne was too 'ot, I shall.'

The guards discussed this radical notion for several moments, then pushed the door wider.

Cheevely stepped hesitantly into the room.

'We could make a run for it,' offered Mignonne.

'Not me,' said Cavendish. 'Look.'

The guards had now opened the door completely and were standing on its threshold with their swords drawn.

Mignonne snorted.

'Talk about overkill,' she said.

Cheevely glanced over his shoulder, sprinted to the other side of the room, and swiftly opened one of the windows.

'There!' he exclaimed, and he and the guards high-tailed it back out to the corridor and closed the door behind them.

The window had not been open very long when a sudden gust of wind blew some of the king's papers onto the floor.

'Now we're in trouble,' Mignonne said.

'Not us,' replied Cavendish sleepily. 'Cheevely.'

'Well *that's* not very fair,' protested Mignonne. '*You* were the one who wanted some fresh air.'

There was another blast of wind, and yet more papers fluttered and glided about until the room was a sea of displaced correspondence.

'You should pick that up,' said Mignonne.

'Why me?' Cavendish grumbled. 'And what's that dreadful racket?'

The two dogs turned towards the window as the heavy beat of wings came to a sudden stop. A raven had landed on the sill and was now preening its feathers. They rustled dryly like expensive silk. The raven tipped its head and perused the scattered papers, gave Cavendish a sharp, disapproving look, and jumped to the floor.

Cavendish hauled himself to his feet and growled.

'No, wait,' Mignonne whispered. 'Let's see what it does.'

The raven hopped closer to the dogs, stretched out its right foot, and cawed.

'Is that supposed to mean something?' Cavendish asked haughtily. 'We don't do bird speak, you know.'

'Forget what it's saying,' said Mignonne quietly. 'Look at its leg.'

Now that the bird had moved into the firelight, something could be seen twinkling on its ankle. Mignonne lowered her head and raised her shoulder blades like a cat on the prowl. She edged forward as close as she dared and studied the bird's foot. Its ankle glinted again. The raven was wearing a miniature bangle.

'What is it?' Cavendish asked.

'Diamonds, I think,' said Mignonne.

She peered at the glittering stones.

'Yes,' she said. 'This bird is wearing diamonds!'

'Preposterous!'

'I do know diamonds when I see them,' Mignonne retorted.

'My mistake,' said Cavendish. 'Of course you do. You have *drawers* of the things.'

Mignonne ignored the gibe and looked more closely at the bird.

'It seems so familiar,' she said. 'It's as though I've seen it before.'

She wondered if it might be the same bird that had circled the king and his horse on the cliffs at Dover, but then dismissed the idea. That had been two years ago now, and a long way from Oxford.

'Don't be ridiculous,' Cavendish guffawed. 'You couldn't possibly know if you've seen it before. There are millions of those birds and they all look exactly the same.'

'No, they don't. Anyway, this one has diamonds and I think that's a sign. Perhaps they mean the raven is special in some way. Is that what it's trying to tell us?'

'No,' said Cavendish. 'They're all thieves. It's stolen the diamonds and probably means to steal from us, too.'

If the raven had understood this insult, it didn't react. Instead it swept its ankle over its chest feathers, turned its back, and hopped across the room. Then it snatched up one of the king's papers in its beak, examined it briefly, and tossed it aside.

'Hey!' Cavendish growled.

Almost immediately, a group of people could be heard hurrying noisily down the passageway outside. The king was coming back, and the queen and their courtiers were with him.

The guards clicked their heels, the door swung open with a flourish, and the royal party swept into the room. And stopped.

'Good heavens,' said the queen.

Cavendish and Mignonne looked soberly at the chaos around them and sank slowly to the ground. They pulled their legs and tails beneath them, rested their noses on their front paws, and tried to look pathetic.

The raven had no such conscience, and flung a few more papers about until its eyes rested on one in particular. It tipped its head and paused.

'It's reading,' Mignonne whispered.

'You're being absurd,' snorted Cavendish as the raven pranced on the paper and picked it up in its beak.

'No I'm not. Watch.'

The bird flew across the room, dropped the paper very deliberately onto the king's desk, and then darted out through the open window.

The king turned.

'Who did this?' he asked the guards.

'Master Cheevely,' one of the guards replied.

'The dogs were barking,' said the other.

'They were too hot, perhaps,' said the queen.

The king sighed.

'You must leave Our Majesties,' he told his courtiers. 'We have housework to do.'

King Charles and Queen Henrietta Maria set about retrieving the most sensitive correspondence. They hunted out the copies of secret letters written and sent to Scotland, Ireland and the continent. They refolded battle plans and lists of armaments and shuffled the more ordinary papers into piles, ready for the secretaries to deal with.

When they'd finished, they sent for a decanter of wine, two glasses and some cheese, and sat down by the fire with their dogs.

'It is more orderly now than it was before,' the queen observed as she admired the neatly stacked papers. 'We should arrange your desk next,' she added. 'It is in a most ugly state.'

'The king's desk!' Mignonne exclaimed. 'They haven't looked at the letter the raven picked up!'

'They hardly even noticed the raven,' Cavendish replied. 'They were too appalled at the mess.'

'Well I want to know what the letter says,' said Mignonne.

She jumped from the queen's knee.

'That bird was searching for something,' she continued, 'and I think it found it.'

'You have a touch of the vapours, dear,' Cavendish teased.

Mignonne took no notice, but trotted purposefully to the king's desk and climbed onto his chair.

'What are you doing, ma petite?' the queen laughed.

Mignonne scanned the top of the desk.

'Oh, pox,' she said to Cavendish. 'This thing's covered in papers. I don't know which one the bird was so interested in.'

'Come here, Mignonne,' called the queen.

Mignonne stepped right into the middle of the desk and sat down.

'No!' the king raised his voice. 'This is too much!'

He strode angrily across the room. Mignonne stood up. The king rounded the desk and smacked her bottom.

'Off!' he said.

'Serves you right,' said Cavendish.

The queen came to rescue Mignonne, but just as she was about to lift her into her arms, she paused.

'But what is this?' she asked as she dragged a letter out from under Mignonne's feet. 'It is from our friend John Williams, Archbishop of York. He writes to warn you about a man named Oliver Cromwell.'

'That? Oh yes,' said the king. 'It arrived a day or so ago. I can't imagine what it's doing here. I thought I'd left it over there,' he added, pointing to a side table. 'For filing.'

The queen read further down the letter.

'Our friend Williams says,' she continued, 'that tho' Cromwell is currently of mean rank and use, he would yet climb higher.'

'He may be right about that,' said the king absentmindedly.

'Is this,' the queen asked through narrowed eyes, 'the same Cromwell? Is this the man who was a farmer and is now a Member of Parliament? Is this the man who believes that he is chosen to fight for God's kingdom?'

'God's kingdom?' the king repeated ironically. 'Aye, madam, so he professes. He was certainly quick to take up arms.'

The king paused and looked up.

'How do you know all this?' he asked, suddenly paying attention.

'Prince Rupert told me,' the queen replied. 'He too, is wary of Cromwell. He tells me that Cromwell's troopers are men of good spirit and discipline, that they are enlisted for their faith, that they are paid promptly...'

She gathered Mignonne up and wandered back to the fire.

'...that they showed fine mettle at Winceby, and are well trained...'

She set Mignonne down, passed her a cheese tit-bit, then turned quickly and glared at the king.

Her eyes were burning.

'This Cromwell man is fearless, Charles!' she cried, beating her fists in the air. 'They say he rode straight at our dragoons even as they reloaded. They shot his horse from under him!'

'But he got up,' said the king. 'More's the pity.'

'You should *heed* our friend's letter,' the queen

implored. 'It gives good advice. You *must* listen to what it says. You must listen to those who love you, Charles. Hear how the letter ends.'

She took a deep breath and began to read aloud.

"My humble motion is, that either you would win Cromwell to you by promises of fair treatment, or catch him by some stratagem, and cut him short."

The queen sighed in exasperation.

'Is this not exactly what I have been saying these past months?' she wailed. 'You must cut *all* your enemies short. They have already taken your navy, your capital, and the armoury at Hull. Now the Scots are crossing the River Tweed to join them. Cut them short, Charles! Cut them short before they cut you!'

CHAPTER FIFTEEN
Bo's House.
The 21st Century

Cavendish chuckled.

'I remember that,' he said. 'The queen was livid!'

'I don't think Mignonne had ever seen her in such a temper,' Bo agreed.

'Well, the king could be pretty infuriating, much as I hate to admit it,' Cavendish replied. 'He had some good advisors, the Archbishop being one of them, but he didn't always listen.'

'Was the Archbishop right?' asked Bo. 'I mean about that Cromwell person.'

'Ohhh, yes,' Cavendish exhaled. 'The Archbishop was spot-on.'

'The raven must have known that,' said Bo. 'It was adamant that the king should read the letter again.'

'It certainly seemed that way,' said Cavendish. 'It could have been chance, I suppose, but she was a clever bird. Goodness knows where she got those diamonds. It was a lady's ring, of course, but it was very old and valuable.'

'How do you know she was a she?' Bo asked.

Cavendish faltered.

'Who?' he asked.

'The bird. You said "she" was clever, "she" got those diamonds.'

'Oh?'

'Come on, Cavendish. Tell me. What do you know about her? Was she the raven I saw at Dover?'

'Possibly,' Cavendish answered eventually. 'Her name was Sioluc. It's the Old English word for silk. If you say it quickly enough it sounds just like it.'

'Did you ever see her again?'

'Ah, now that I cannot tell you.'

Bo stamped a foot.

'Cavendish!' she exclaimed. 'Sometimes you're even more exasperating than the king himself!'

'Like master, like dog,' Cavendish winked. 'What I will tell you is that *Mignonne* saw Sioluc again, and quite soon. It happened at Exeter.'

'Exeter?' Bo repeated. 'What was Mignonne doing in Exeter?'

'She went there with the queen,' Cavendish replied. 'Exeter was in the heart of Royalist country, and the safest place for the queen to have her new baby.'

CHAPTER SIXTEEN
Bedford House, Exeter, England.
June 1644

Baby Hetty-Anne was lying in the queen's arms and looking tiny against the huge four-poster bed with all its tassels and drapes and acres of lace. She was tightly wrapped in swaddling clothes, and was wearing a cotton bonnet which was a little too large and had slipped jauntily over one eye.

Mignonne jumped up beside her.

'Look, chérie,' said the queen as she adjusted the bonnet. 'Here is Mignonne! She has a collar set with sapphires. They are like your eyes, non? Mignonne will take care of you when maman is gone to France.'

'Gone to France?' Mignonne fretted. 'What do you mean, gone to France? What are you talking about?'

She clambered over the baby and snuggled into the crook of the queen's free arm.

'I know,' said Henrietta Maria as her fingers toyed with Mignonne's fur. 'But I must leave. The king's enemies are searching for me. I hear they may be within a few miles of here. If they were to find me...'

She shuddered, and Mignonne pawed at her hand.

'I am unwell, Mignonne. My arms and legs are cold and my sight has gone from one eye. At times I feel I am a person poisoned.'

'I do not want to travel,' she sobbed. 'I do not want to leave my babies. But I must. If I do not leave, the king himself may try to come here. His affection for me would make him risk everything, and I cannot allow that.'

Huge tears rolled out of her big brown eyes, tumbled over her necklace, and dropped into the folds of her gown.

'Soon,' she whispered, holding a finger to her lips. 'I will go to Falmouth. From there I will sail to France. And you know the worst thing, Mignonne? The worst thing...'

Mignonne scrabbled under a pillow and pressed it hard against her ears. She didn't think she wanted to hear the worst thing, but she heard it anyway.

'I think that I shall never see the king again!'

The queen then howled so loudly, and in such terrible anguish, that Mignonne and the baby joined in with her, and physicians and maids all rushed into the room to see what was amiss.

Mignonne was taken outside where she made straight for the shade of a yew tree and flopped onto the grass. With her chin resting on her front paws, she moved her eyes from side to side and looked about.

She and her mistress had spent many afternoons together in this lovely garden. The queen had read books or written letters, and Mignonne had dozed peacefully beside her. Those had been happy times, but for most of her days in Exeter, Henrietta Maria had been unwell, miserable and worried about her family.

She knew that Princess Mary was safe enough, since she was still in Holland. And though Elizabeth and Henry were in the hands of Parliament in London, they were well-cared for. But her husband and two eldest sons were in the front line of battle. They could be captured or killed at any moment and, with the country in such turmoil, there was no hope of any reunion soon.

For weeks now, Mignonne had tried desperately to distract the queen and cheer her up.

She'd swung from the maids' skirts until the girls had squealed and kicked out. She'd bounced on Henrietta Maria's bed, taken the eiderdown in her teeth, and shaken it furiously until feathers flew. She'd dug holes in the lawn and searched for imaginary treasures with her nose, then hared back to the house with a muddy snout. And if a footman or a lady-in-waiting had tried to stop her antics, she'd sat obediently when told, but then run around in circles just as they were about to grab her.

The queen had laughed, sometimes, but Mignonne's efforts had come to nought. She was exhausted, the war had torn her family apart, and now her beloved mistress was talking about leaving the country and never coming back.

Things had to be really bad for the queen to do that, she loved her husband and children so much. But she could trust no one, and though Mignonne hated to admit it, she was beginning to feel the same way herself. It

wasn't in her nature to be suspicious of people, but how could she be anything else? People were suspicious of each other.

It was understandable. Mignonne had overheard enough conversations to know what a treacherous, spiteful sort of war this was. It had made everyone wary. The enemy weren't foreigners in some distant land. They were fellow Englishmen, and they didn't always show themselves. That was the frightening thing. The two sides lived cheek by jowl, often without realising it. Yet, whilst no one could be certain of their neighbour's true loyalties, they might be well aware that their own brother or father supported the opposite cause.

The servants at Bedford House had even talked about a local family who'd eaten supper together one night and then gone out the following morning with every intention of shooting each other, should it have come to that. And because the Roundheads and Royalists were evenly matched, there seemed to be no end in sight. Defeat followed victory followed defeat for them both. Towns and castles were taken by one faction, then snatched back by the other, over and over again. The fighting, and the resulting poverty, disease and distress just went on multiplying.

Mignonne thumped her nose on the ground.

'I hate this war,' she growled. 'I hate it, hate it, *hate* it!'

Fed up, depressed, and drained by her thoughts, she dozed off in the fading sun.

She was woken by a dreadful screeching and sat up quickly to see a raven and a gull hopping about in circles on the lawn. They were face to face, gaping their beaks and jabbing at each other's chests with their taloned feet.

As Mignonne watched them, something caught her eye.

Every time the raven jabbed, its right ankle glinted.

Mignonne stood up to take a closer look but, as she approached the birds, they leapt into the air in a particularly nasty bout of aggression, and she retreated. Eventually, amid a noisy clashing of wings and a great many flying feathers, the gull seemed to give up. It squawked furiously at the raven and flew away.

The raven watched it go, opened its own wings to check for damage, then folded them back and smoothed them down with its beak. When it was satisfied that all was well, it hopped towards Mignonne who lay down to examine its ankle. Sure enough, there was the circle of diamonds.

Mignonne barked.

'You're the raven from Oxford,' she declared. 'Were you at Dover, too? What are you doing *here*?'

Sioluc brushed her diamonds over her chest feathers and cawed. Then she turned, took a few swift strides, and glided away.

She circled several times before coming to land at the very end of the garden, not on the lawn, but at the top of an unruly clambering rose. She had her back to Mignonne,

and was leaning over and watching something intently.
Mignonne got up and went to investigate.

CHAPTER SEVENTEEN

Away from the house, the manicured gardens petered into a tangle of bramble bushes, tall nettles and willowherb. The rose grew through these and over the roof of a shed. This was where Sioluc was sitting.

Mignonne negotiated her way past the nettles to the base of the brambles. They had the unmistakable stench of fox, and Mignonne was certain that there'd be a hole somewhere which the fox had made or enlarged to get through them.

Mignonne padded backwards and forwards, hunting for the hole. When she found it, she lay flat on her stomach and peered into it. She could see a clear space between the back of the brambles and the rear of the shed. She couldn't tell whether there was enough room for her to stand upright in this space, but at least she'd be able to turn around. That was important. She didn't want to have to reverse out.

She edged forward and began to negotiate her way into the hole. She knew from bitter experience that it was vital to take it easy and not struggle against the brambles' springy stems. Do that, and they would catch hold of her fur.

With her legs tucked underneath her, and her body kept low to the ground, she pawed her way gingerly past the brambles and into the clearing.

Once safely through, she breathed a sigh of relief. There was ample room for her to stand. In fact, other than for a canopy of rose, the space was almost open to the sky.

She straightened up, shook herself, and looked about.

The shed was made of wood and was seriously rotten. Mignonne was wondering how it was still in one piece when the chinks between its boards filled with a thin orange light. She sniffed the air and caught a whiff of tallow. Someone had entered the shed with a lighted a lantern.

A man spoke in a low voice. His accent was strong, but Mignonne had heard it many times before, especially since she'd arrived in Exeter.

'It will be day after next,' he said. 'At dawn most like. Just 'er an' the physician, plus a lady wot waits. Best tarry 'til they's gone a few mile. Then waylay them on the road. Tread careful, mind, for she's poorly and we need to get 'er alive. Be sure thee do that, mind. Queen'll do us no good if she's gorn dead.'

Mignonne's lower jaw dropped wide open. She couldn't believe what she was hearing. Worse still, it wasn't just the man's accent that was familiar. She also recognised his voice.

She wanted to warn her mistress about this new

danger, though she had no idea how to do it. She began to bark, but then decided no one would hear her. She would have to run to the house. She knew she didn't have time to lie down and wriggle carefully past the brambles, she'd have to dash through them as fast as she could and hope they didn't snag her.

She had just taken a deep breath to prepare herself when she heard a dry rustle. She leant back on her haunches and glanced up, expecting to see the raven, but there was no sign of it. Instead she saw the gull from the fight. It had landed on the rose and was now climbing down the gnarled branches towards her.

She barked at it and, with a beating of wings and a shower of falling petals and leaves, it landed briefly beside her and took off again. She whipped round, but in the split second it took her to notice its gaping beak and sharp orange tongue, it had thrust out its huge feet and come straight at her. She saw the flesh-coloured webbing stretched taut between its talons and felt a searing pain streak across her back. She ducked and heard the gull turn, but whilst it was still above her and before it could make contact again, there was a quick flash of black and a terrible scream. The gull's soft underbelly parted in a spray of thick, warm blood and it crashed into the back of the shed and fell to the ground, dead.

The force of the blow was too much for the shed. Even as Mignonne was shaking off the gull's blood, the rotting timbers groaned and creaked and a whole section of them collapsed in a cloud of dust.

Mignonne turned to her rescuer.

'Where did you come from?' she asked Sioluc. 'Last time I saw you, you were sitting on the roof.'

The raven dipped her head.

'Well, anyway, thank you,' Mignonne added with a nod to the gull. 'I don't know what got into it, but as soon as I started barking, it attacked me. And now I have to go. I need to warn my mistress about something, if I can get back through those blasted brambles.'

Sioluc nodded and headed for the foxhole as though to guide Mignonne through it.

'Thank you,' said Mignonne again, 'Ow!'

She'd been grabbed from behind and caught firmly by the tail.

She squealed, then wriggled and flipped like a landed fish and squealed again.

'Shut thar noise!' a man whispered hoarsely. 'Shut it, d'ye hear?'

He let go of Mignonne's tail, but then kicked her on her bottom.

'Go orn,' he said. 'Out! That-a-way.'

Mignonne clambered blindly over the fallen timbers, through a doorway on the far side of the shed, and into a paved area, some long-forgotten part of the garden. The man and Sioluc followed, and the raven settled on a mossy statue.

Another man appeared, swinging an extinguished lantern. This was the owner of the voice that Mignonne had recognised. She'd hoped she was wrong, unlikely though that was. She had a good ear for a familiar voice. Now she stared at the man with utter contempt.

He was the footman from London, Edmund Smales.

'Anyone 'eard the noise?' he asked.

'Be a damn miracle if they 'aven't. Right crash, it were,' replied the other man.

'Then thee'd best go quick. 'Case someone comes,' said Smales.

'Aye,' the first man agreed. 'Day after, you say. At dawn?'

Smales mumbled an affirmative and the man turned to leave, but as he did so he noticed the sapphires in Mignonne's collar.

'Them's no real, surely?' he spluttered as he bent to take a closer look.

Mignonne shrank away from him.

'Prob'ly,' Smales replied.

'Then I'll 'ave 'em,' said the man. 'I'll 'ave to kill 'im, 'course. Can't let 'im go home with no collar. They'd know someone's been here. Best he disappears.'

'She,' said Smales.

'What?'

'*She*. He's a she,' Smales explained. 'Thee'll 'ave to kill *her*.'

'Wha'd'you care?' asked the other man suspiciously.

'I don't,' said Smales. 'I'm just saying, that's all.'

The man grabbed Mignonne by the scruff of her neck and flung her upwards, then pinned her against his chest with one arm. He reached out with the other and waggled his fingers at Smales.

'Hassen thee a knife?' he asked. 'I'll cut 'er throat.'

Mignonne yelped and struggled to free herself, but

the man only tightened his grasp, which squeezed her rib-cage and knocked the wind from her lungs.

'Don' you be mad, now. She's only a dog,' Smales replied.

'Tha's what I means. Only a dog.'

Mignonne felt hot liquid rush between her hind legs.

'Oh Gad, she's gone peed 'erself now,' the man said. 'Pathetic rafty lapdog.'

He laid his free hand against Mignonne's throat.

'Best leave 'er,' said Smales with remarkable calm. ''Twill only mess our plans. Queen'll make a rumpus and put her trip back, for she won't go nowhere 'til 'er dog's found.'

'Then we'll 'ave to make it easy,' the man replied as he put pressure on Mignonne's neck. 'Leave the body where it'll be quickly seen,' he added. 'On the lawn or summat.'

Smales took a step forward.

'You put 'er down now,' he ordered. 'Put 'er down or I'll…'

Mignonne had never encountered a raven in full flight. She had no concept of Sioluc's massive wingspan and how frightening it could be. Neither, apparently, had her captor, and when Sioluc flew straight at him and everything around him went black, he threw his hands to his face and flung Mignonne sideways. She hit the corner of the shed, slid down it and landed in a heap.

Meanwhile, Edmund Smales made the most of Sioluc's intervention. He lunged forward, swung the lantern with all his might and slammed it against the back of the other man's knees with a sickening thud. The man crumpled and Smales hit him again. This time the man groaned and sprawled face down on the ground.

Smales then tossed the lantern aside, picked up a trembling Mignonne and carried her back through the partially demolished shed. Sioluc followed. When Smales reached the clearing, he stepped over the dead body of the gull, set Mignonne down and pulled a knife from his waistband.

Mignonne yelped hoarsely and tried yet again to reach the gap in the brambles, but to her horror Sioluc opened her wings and blocked her path.

She was cornered.

Smales raised the knife and Mignonne flattened herself against the warm summer earth and waited for the first slash.

Nothing happened.

She rolled her eyes upwards.

Smales had removed his jacket and was now wrapping it around his left hand. That done, he used the improvised gauntlet to bend back the brambles, took the knife in his other hand, and began to hack frantically at the brambles' springy stems.

''Tis vicious stuff, this,' he puffed, suddenly dropping his broad accent. 'And all bloodied up. As are you, Mignonne. What was all that about, then? Upsetting birds? That's not like you.'

He quickly cut a pathway out of the clearing, then scooped Mignonne up and, with Sioluc swooping and diving alongside, galloped across the lawns. At the back door to the house, he sped past the guards, who did nothing to stop him, then through the hall, up the stairs and along a passageway.

Finally, he flung open the door to the queen's bedroom.

CHAPTER EIGHTEEN

Her Majesty was propped against a mountain of pillows.

Her doctor was sitting in a nearby chair, and Hetty-Anne was asleep in her arms.

'Mon dieu!' the queen exclaimed.

'Out! Out! Out!' screamed the doctor.

'No, listen, Your Majesty, I beg of you,' Smales pleaded breathlessly and still devoid of his accent.

He held Mignonne aloft, and the queen gasped and laid her baby aside.

'Mignonne! But what has happened?' she cried, struggling out of bed. 'The blood!'

'Most of it is not her own,' Smales explained kindly. 'But she does have a nasty scratch on her back, from brambles, I think. Or possibly a gull.'

Right on cue, Mignonne howled pathetically.

'A gull? Oh ma pauvre petite!' the queen wailed in sympathy. 'Alors,' she added, climbing back under the covers and tapping them with her fingers, 'put her here.'

Smales passed Mignonne to the doctor who examined her wound and then laid her beside the queen.

'But what has happened?' the queen asked again.

'And why is there a raven in my bed-chamber?'

She peered at Smales.

'You were in our service at London, were you not?' she asked him.

'Yes, ma'am. Please, you must quit this place. Now. Tonight.'

'But I cannot leave! I have a new baby!' the queen replied as though appalled at the very suggestion.

'Yet you planned to make for Falmouth tomorrow,' said Smales.

The queen took a short breath.

'Is that not so, Ma'am?' Smales persisted.

'Go on,' said the queen warily.

'There is a plot to kidnap you,' Smales continued. 'The plotters believe I am one of their number. I am not. On the contrary, I am a Royalist spy. As such, I have a duty to mislead your enemies. I had succeeded in doing just that by giving their messenger false information about your plans when we were disturbed. Mignonne began to bark, and a gull collided with our meeting place.'

'And with Mignonne, also?'

'I don't know. Whatever the circumstances, the bird died. The messenger went to see what had happened, caught Mignonne and saw her collar. He was all set to kill her for its jewels.'

'Then I hope you killed him, instead!' exclaimed the doctor.

'No,' said Smales. 'I had to let him go. Had I not, his fellow plotters would have come to look for him. If they had found him dead...'

'...there would have been no hope for my escape?' asked the queen.

Smales nodded.

'They would have stayed to watch the house,' he said. 'As it is, the man is but stunned, and will make his rendezvous. Yet he must suspect my actions. He will be back to put a watch on the house anyway, and he will not be alone. That may happen within the hour, two at most. You must go, your Majesty. You must go, and go now. If you do not...'

'We shall have to begin all over again?'

'Yes, ma'am,' Smales replied. 'And that could be very perilous indeed.'

'I can trust no one,' the queen said miserably. 'I know that. But you have saved Mignonne, and brought her home to me.'

She stroked Mignonne's back.

'It may be a trick, perhaps,' she continued thoughtfully. 'But it is a very risky one. Risky because you have shown your face. Are you prepared to die for the cause you believe in?'

'Yes, ma'am,' came the answer.

'And what is that cause, pray?'

'His Majesty The King, ma'am.'

The queen toyed with Mignonne's fur and glanced at Hetty-Anne, who was now cradled in the doctor's arms.

'The king,' she whispered to herself. 'Dieu et mon droit, my dearest Charles.'

She turned to her doctor.

'Call the guards,' she said calmly.

111

When the guards arrived, the queen gave them specific instructions.

'You will keep this man in irons until you have word that I am safely in France,' she told them. 'But,' she added, raising a hand, 'he is absolutely not to be harmed in your custody. If he is lying, then we shall know it soon enough and the king will decide his fate. If he is telling the truth, then he will be out of the clutches of these wicked men until a place of safety can be found for him. And that is as it should be. For he has saved the life of Mignonne, and perhaps of me also.'

She looked steadily at Smales.

'We will see,' she said.

Within less than an hour, she was ready to leave. The journey she was about to make was tedious and uncomfortable at the best of times, but she was weak and unwell, and the countryside was riddled with enemy spies and Roundhead soldiers, all of whom were out to catch her. Even if Smales had been telling the truth, there were still many hazards to overcome.

Mignonne decided to hide in the carriage and go to France too, but the queen knew her too well. She hadn't even got out of bed before she'd called for a footman and ordered him to put Mignonne on a lead. On no account, she'd stressed formidably, was Mignonne to be allowed to stow away.

When the queen had settled herself into the carriage, she asked the footman to pass Mignonne to her. For a brief moment Mignonne thought she might be going to France after all, but the queen sat her upright on her knee and looked into her eyes.

'You must go back to Oxford, ma petite,' she said in a trembling voice. 'You must return to the king.'

She brushed a tear-stained cheek against Mignonne's fur, then nodded to the footman to lift her dog away.

As a few last adjustments were made to the queen's coach, Mignonne sat on the steps to the house. There she was joined by Sioluc, who settled companionably beside her.

Mignonne thought about how the raven had perched on the roof of the shed. It was as though it had known about the meeting between Smales and the other man, and had been there to witness it. She concluded that, since the raven was obviously a Royalist, Smales must be one too. She wasn't sure what the gull had had to do with it all, but that hardly mattered now. She just hoped and prayed she was right about Smales, otherwise there'd be real trouble.

The coachman snapped his reins, and Mignonne snapped out of her reverie. The horses walked forward, the wheels of the coach crunched on the gravel, and Mignonne caught a final glimpse of her mistress's pale face.

Mignonne and Sioluc sat together and watched the carriage disappear from view. Then Sioluc spread her wings and rose into the air. She hovered briefly above Mignonne's head and cawed a farewell before she, like the queen, flew into the night.

CHAPTER NINETEEN
Bo's House.
The 21st Century

'Do you think those men came to watch the house?' asked Bo.

'I'm sure they did,' Cavendish replied. 'But they wouldn't have stayed very long. They'd have given up when they realised the queen had gone.'

'And Mignonne? How long did Mignonne stay?'

'Another week,' said Cavendish. 'She spent most of it lying beside Hetty-Anne's cradle. But she was behaving very strangely. When she finally went back to Oxford, a letter to the king went with her, describing her symptoms. It told how she'd been twitching and trembling and making harsh crying noises in her sleep. When she walked it was with a curious hopping gait.'

'Maybe she had a sore paw or something,' Bo suggested. 'Or maybe it was the aftereffect of the gull's attack.'

'Maybe,' Cavendish agreed. 'But there was more. She'd try to nibble the fur on her back, or lift a foreleg and bury her head underneath it. Sometimes she was seen to stretch out a leg, spread her toes apart, then sweep them across her chest.'

'She must have been miserable,' said Bo. 'Just imagine it. She had no friends at Exeter, and now the queen had left her behind. She must have been half-mad with grief and loneliness.'

'And that's what her behaviour was put down to. Everyone thought she was pining, which of course she was. But there was more to it than that, and when she got back to Oxford, she told me all about it. She said she'd heard voices. They'd bantered and boasted about how they would find the queen, chop off her head, and carry it to London...'

'She was having bad dreams. It's hardly surprising.'

'...she said she'd seen how close they'd come to doing exactly what they threatened, how sometimes all that stood between Henrietta Maria and capture was a couple of fields and a dirt track.'

'She was imagining the worst.'

Cavendish nodded.

'But wait,' he said. 'When Mignonne set out with Smales and a party of guards on the long road back to Oxford, the visions continued. She saw the queen arrive at Falmouth and board a ship, part of a small fleet. It headed down the estuary towards the English Channel but was chased and harried by Parliament ships firing cannon. Then, at last, the silhouette of a different fleet rose over the horizon. Its ensigns were French, and when the Parliament ships saw them, they turned back, and the queen sailed on.'

'Is that true? Is that what really happened?' asked

Bo.

'Yes,' Cavendish replied. 'The queen was safe. Mignonne continued towards Oxford and, five days into her journey, her visions stopped just as suddenly as they'd begun, and a raven appeared.'

'Sioluc?'

'The very same,' said Cavendish. 'Though of course Mignonne didn't know her by name. Sioluc was thin and bedraggled, but Mignonne wasn't surprised. She knew, somehow, that the bird had followed the queen all the way to France. When Sioluc held out her diamond bracelet and cawed, Mignonne realised that the journey had had a happy outcome.'

'So the visions Mignonne had...' pondered Bo.

'Were instinct, perhaps?' suggested Cavendish. 'Some sort of sixth sense? We animals have a talent for that.'

'You mean like the way I know my mistress is coming home long before she actually gets here?'

'Exactly.'

'But what about the details? The soldiers, Falmouth, the ships?'

'Mignonne had seen plenty of soldiers. She'd been to Dover, too. She knew what ships and harbours looked like.'

'Even so.'

'There was certainly something very strange about it all,' Cavendish agreed. 'Still, Mignonne was soon back to her old self, especially when letters from the queen began to arrive.'

'So Smales really was a Royalist...'

'Through and through,' Cavendish replied. 'He was a double agent, and a good one, at that. He'd convinced the Parliamentarians he was working for them, and they thought their dreams had come true. After all, what could be better than having a palace footman as their "mole"? They even fell for that terrible accent of his. They thought he came from the West Country, the very heart of royalism. But they'd got Smales badly wrong. Little did they know that he would be rewarded by the king himself for what he'd done at Exeter. He'd saved Mignonne's life, and probably the queen's as well. The king found him somewhere safe to stay so he could lie low for a while, just in case he'd been rumbled, but after a while he returned to London to continue his good work.'

'Oh that's a pity,' said Bo.

'How's that?"

'Because I liked him. I mean Mignonne liked him, and now I don't suppose she'll ever see him again, what with him gone to London and her being back in Oxford.'

'Mignonne didn't stay in Oxford forever,' Cavendish replied. 'She returned to London, too.'

CHAPTER TWENTY
The Deanery, Christ Church, Oxford.
26 April 1646

Mignonne and Cavendish were waiting in the king's study. Beside them was a canvas saddlebag. It contained a small blanket, a water bottle and dish, some dog biscuits and Mignonne's lead. The last of these was made from plain bridle leather, and matched her collar. Neither were jewelled and nothing about them gave a clue to their ownership.

'I don't want to go,' Mignonne whimpered.

'I don't want you to go either,' Cavendish replied miserably. 'But at least you'll have Elizabeth and Henry to play with. I'll be cooped up in Newcastle whilst the king has endless meeting with the Scots.'

'But Elizabeth and Henry haven't seen me for more than four years!' Mignonne wailed. 'They probably won't even know who I am. I'd rather go to Newcastle.'

'No, Mignonne, you can't do that. You must go back to London. Elizabeth will remember you, and you'll soon make friends with Henry. Edmund Smales will be there, too, and Old Sowerbutts the gardener. You used to like him. He fed you special biscuits.'

'Oh, yes. So he did,' said Mignonne without a trace of enthusiasm. 'But that won't be any consolation if I never see you again.'

'Of course you'll see me again,' said Cavendish.

He laid a paw on Mignonne's back.

'Of course you will.'

He tipped his head and twitched an ear.

'Listen,' he said. 'The king and Prince Rupert are coming to say good bye.'

King Charles and his nephew entered the study and sat down, and Rupert hoisted Mignonne onto his knee. He'd always had a soft spot for her, and she for him, but they'd become even closer since Rupert's own poodle, Boy, had been killed at the Battle of Marston Moor. The battle had been a bad defeat for the Royalists and, ever since that day, rumours had spread that Prince Rupert's military luck had died with his dog.

Now it was beginning to look as though the rumours were right. The Royalist cause had taken a turn for the worse. More battles had been lost, and the king's secret correspondence to Catholic countries like Spain and Ireland had been captured at Naseby. The king's enemies had been cock-a-hoop at that one. They'd said the letters 'proved' he was trying to convert England to Catholicism.

Meanwhile, Oliver Cromwell had made himself General of Horse and taken the city of Bristol in the west country. He and his Roundhead soldiers were now swarming over the Royalists' last remaining stronghold, and the king's eldest son and heir, Prince Charles, had fled abroad.

In spite of these setbacks, King Charles was not about to give up. He still thought he could strike a deal with the Scots, and was about to ride north to see them. He was taking Cavendish with him, but Mignonne was being sent to London.

Mignonne sat quietly whilst Prince Rupert removed her lead from the saddle-bag.

'You are to ride with Sir William,' he said gently as he clipped the lead onto her collar. 'He is a fine young man and will take best care of you. Now then,' he added, 'this is for you.'

He undid the top two buttons of his doublet, reached inside, and produced a scarlet ribbon.

'Remember this?' he asked. 'It is the ribbon I lent you at Edgehill. I have not worn it since, but have kept it for such a moment as this. Methinks now I *should* have worn it. Perhaps it would have brought me better luck.'

He unravelled the ribbon and tied it around Mignonne's neck.

'It is a very fine ribbon,' said the king, leaning forward to pat Mignonne's head. 'A very fine ribbon for a very fine dog. And now, I fear, it is time for you to leave. Princess Elizabeth will be happy to see you. She is so lonely, you know. You will make a good companion for her. It is the queen's wish, Mignonne, and mine, too.'

Mignonne slipped to the floor.

'Don't let them do this to me,' she pleaded with

Cavendish. 'Please don't let them send me away!'

'How can I stop them?' her friend replied. 'I'll think of you. More than you can imagine. And you in turn must try to think of the children. Your duty now is to them, particularly Elizabeth.'

'But I don't want duty. I want to stay with you.'

Cavendish stood up and rested his head on Mignonne's shoulder.

'You are a royal dog, Mignonne,' he said. 'That is a great privilege, but it comes with responsibilities and more ties than Prince Rupert's pretty ribbon. I know it's hard, but you are Elizabeth's dog now. And you would hate Newcastle, believe me. I hear it rains all the time, and that the north wind blows like a boar's bum.'

Mignonne giggled.

'There, that's my girl,' said Cavendish.

'Summon Sir William,' called the king.

CHAPTER TWENTY-ONE
Bo's House.
The 21st Century

'What *was* Newcastle like?' Bo asked Cavendish. 'Did it really rain all the time?'

'Not *all* the time, but it wasn't the best eight months of my life. When the king wasn't having boring talks with the Scots he was dragging me over a golf course. He was a big fan of golf. I never understood its appeal, personally.'

'And did the talks work? No,' said Bo. 'I can see by your face that they didn't.'

'The Scots tried to make the king accept their church. Even the queen thought he should do what they wanted. But the king still wouldn't give in, so the Scots handed him over to the Parliamentarians.'

'So that was that, I suppose,' said Bo. 'The Parliamentarians had got their way.'

'Not quite,' Cavendish replied. 'They were starting to squabble amongst themselves, not least because their soldiers hadn't been paid and were running amok and looting everything in sight. Some thought they should disband the army, but of course Cromwell wouldn't hear of it. He loved his army. He wasn't about to admit he'd created a monster, so he did something else instead. Early one morning, he sent five hundred of his troopers to the house where Parliament were keeping me and the king. I remember hearing them approach, and the way their horses' hooves thundered over the ground. The king was asleep, but I ran to the window and looked out. I could see they were Cromwell's men. I knew what was about to happen. They woke my master up and took us both away. From that day forth we were no longer prisoners of Parliament, but of Oliver Cromwell and his men.'

There was something so final about Cavendish's tone that for a few moments Bo couldn't think of anything to say.

'Did you ever meet Cromwell?' she eventually asked.

'Twice,' said Cavendish quietly. 'I don't remember much about the first time. It was just after he took us prisoner, but it was very brief. The second time was at an inn in Maidenhead. I think I was more angry than afraid.'

'Was Mignonne there?' Bo wondered aloud. 'No, stupid,' she answered her own question. 'Of course she wasn't. She wouldn't have been invited.'

'Quite,' said Cavendish.

CHAPTER TWENTY-TWO
St James's Palace, London.
July 1647

Mignonne was sitting by a window in the salon, admiring her reflection. Apart from watching herself, and the way her opal collar gleamed in the sunshine, she was also keeping an eye on the room behind her.

In its centre was seven-year-old Prince Henry, who was brushing up his swordsmanship with a length of wood. He didn't seem to have noticed that the 'enemy', once a cushion, had well and truly surrendered. Its silk cover lay in shreds, and most of its insides, thousands of tiny white feathers, were strewn across the floor or floating in the air.

Sitting close beside Mignonne was Princess Elizabeth, a pretty, rather delicate girl of twelve. Everyone had predicted that she and Mignonne would become friends, and they'd been right. The queen's daughter and poodle were inseparable.

The princess had been doing her needlework, and was now searching through a big bunch of coloured wools. She selected a hank and held it against the partially finished canvas.

'Tch. I don't know, I really don't,' she muttered to herself.

And then louder.

'What do you think, James? Do look. Shall it be this bronze? Or something paler. The beige, perhaps. No. It does not complement the rest. The black? Do help me choose, brother.'

James was curled up against the casement of the window next along, reading a book. He was an affable young man, not yet fourteen, and had fought bravely in the war until he and Prince Rupert had been captured. Rupert had been sent into exile on the continent, but James had joined Henry and Elizabeth in London.

All three children were now prisoners of Parliament, and under house arrest, but they still had cause for optimism. They knew that everyone had grown tired of the war and its hardships. People wanted a return to the old days, and even those who'd been most against the king were beginning to say that having him back might not be such a bad thing.

If only he would stop being so stubborn and start negotiating with Parliament, he might yet be returned to his throne. But for the moment he was a prisoner of Cromwell, and was living at a house in Oxfordshire, which was miles away from any of his family, especially those who'd gone abroad.

The queen, Princess Mary, Prince Charles, Prince Rupert and Baby Hetty-Anne were all overseas now. Hetty-Anne had been smuggled there and Prince Charles had escaped, though without his pageboy, Richard

Cheevely. Cheevely had disappeared on the very night that Charles had sailed to the Scilly Islands. Charles had later written to James to say he couldn't understand why Cheevely should do such a thing, apart from the fact that he'd always said he mistrusted the sea.

When James had read the letter out loud to Elizabeth, Mignonne hadn't been at all surprised at Cheevely's behaviour. Even she, who *liked* the sea, had no desire to get into it, not even on a boat. And anyway, she couldn't imagine Cheevely abroad. She'd heard the queen speaking French, she even understood some of the words, but it still sounded peculiar. As did France and Holland, which the queen had often spoken about. No, Mignonne had decided, Cheevely was not an abroad sort of person.

Elizabeth and James had grown close since James's return. The two of them would often sit huddled together and talk to each other in low whispers. Sometimes they were so secretive that even Mignonne couldn't hear what they were saying, and had to jump up beside them to make it out.

Even so, Mignonne didn't think the prince would be interested in his sister's needlework, so she was surprised when he put down his reading, walked up to Elizabeth, and leant over her shoulder.

'The black,' he said, 'but do look outside. They are preparing a coach. You see?'

Mignonne had been so busy watching the reflections of herself and the things behind her that she hadn't noticed what was happening on the other side of the window. Now she shuffled forward on her bottom and pressed her nose to the glass.

Sure enough, there was a great deal of toing and froing in the courtyard below. Six shining bay horses had been harnessed to one of His Majesty's coaches, and two footmen were spreading its seats with rugs and cushions.

'For whom?' asked Elizabeth. 'For whom do you suppose...'

At that moment the door to the salon opened, and one of the children's nurses appeared with two Roundhead guards and Edmund Smales.

'Good news, children!' the nurse exclaimed as she bustled across the room. 'My word! Where have all these feathers come from?'

She took Henry by his free hand.

'Give me the sword, Henry,' she said as she wrestled the piece of wood away. 'You are to visit your father, this very day!'

The children looked at one another.

'Come! Come, children. Make haste!' she fussed.

'Is it really true?' asked James.

'We are to see father?' added Elizabeth.

'*Who?*' demanded Henry.

'Your father,' the nurse replied. 'Quickly now. Your cloaks are already in the coach, and there is no time to lose. Come, come. The coachman will take you.'

'To where, exactly?' James asked warily.

'To the Greyhound Inn at Maidenhead,' said the

nurse briskly.

Elizabeth picked Mignonne up.

'Mignonne shall come too, shall she not? To see papa?' she asked. 'He is so very fond of her.'

'No. Mignonne will remain at home,' came the firm reply.

The nurse motioned to Smales.

'Take Mignonne into the garden,' she ordered.

'No,' said Elizabeth, stamping her foot as Mignonne squirmed and wriggled in her arms. 'Let her stay here. She likes to look out of the window. She can watch us leave and await our return.'

She placed Mignonne defiantly on the window seat and the nurse huffed and rolled her eyes.

'Very well,' she said haughtily.

She pointed to the door and made a sweeping gesture with one arm, and the children filed out of the room. She and the guards followed them and, as their footsteps receded down the hall, Smales walked up to Mignonne and sat beside her.

'We'll watch together,' he said kindly, 'then I'll take you outside. See if we can't find old Sowerbutts and his biscuits.'

'Tempting,' thought Mignonne, 'but no contest.'

She glanced at the door. The guards had left it wide open, but timing was everything. Too soon, and Smales might catch her. Too late, and the carriage doors would be closed. She waited until Smales turned to look out of the window, then she gave him an apologetic yap and raced for the door. Her nails skittered on the wooden floor as she bounded down the hall. She soon had the children in her sights again, but then they rounded the corner at the end of the gallery and started down the steps to the courtyard.

Mignonne galloped on. She could tell without looking back that Smales hadn't followed her, but then she hadn't expected he would. He was a friend, after all. The guards, though, were an entirely different matter.

She reached the top of the courtyard steps and paused briefly to assess her chances. The nurse was on the other side of the coach, settling the children into it. The guards were on its nearside, and a bit too close for comfort.

Mignonne sped halfway down the steps, then skidded sharp left and followed an arc which brought her, not to the coach, but to its front pair of horses.

She stood on her hind legs and barked.

The coachman half rose, chuckled, and tapped his forefinger against his nose. Mignonne nodded and barked again, then scooted to the farthest side of the coach. The nurse had now finished her fussing, and was standing back to allow one of the footman to close the door. With split-second timing and an almighty effort, Mignonne launched herself through the narrowing gap, slithered into the coach, and dived under one of its seats.

The nurse hammered on the door and tried to open it. 'Hold up! Hold up!' she shouted.

But the coachman, who'd always been a favourite of the queen, and therefore of Mignonne, seemed suddenly to have turned stone-deaf. He snapped his reins purposefully, the six bays lurched forward, and the wheels began to roll with the nurse still hanging onto the door handle, still shouting.

Eventually the nurse had to let go, but even so, and in spite of the children's urgent pleas, Mignonne couldn't be persuaded out from under the seat until she felt sure that the coach had gone too far to turn back.

Only then did she creep out and jump onto Elizabeth's lap.

'Here she is!' laughed James.

'Oh Mignonne!' Elizabeth squealed. 'We are to see papa! At an *inn*! I *knew* you would come too! Do you think Cavendish might be there? You would like to see him, would you not?'

Mignonne hadn't thought about that. Now she was really pleased she'd made it to the coach.

'Who's Cavendish?' asked Henry.

'Why, *papa's* dog, of course,' James replied.

'And who's *papa*?'

'Don't you remember?' Elizabeth asked gently. 'He is the king.'

'Papa left London more than five and a half years ago, Liz,' said James. 'Henry barely knows him.'

'Then Henry has a treat in store,' said Elizabeth.

CHAPTER TWENTY-THREE
The Greyhound Inn, Maidenhead, England.
Later that day

Before the outbreak of the war, the Greyhound Inn at Maidenhead had been a bustling, vibrant place, so well-known for its wealthy clientele that highwaymen had lurked in the surrounding woods, waiting to pounce on them.

On an average day, and if they'd managed to avoid being ambushed, eighty or more coaches had pulled up at the inn. Some of these vehicles had been magnificent, with teams of horses in fabulous harnesses, coachmen and postilions wearing uniforms decorated with gold, and retinues of outriders with specially-bred spotted dogs. Whilst the horses were watered or exchanged for fresh ones, the coaches' passengers would have spilled out, dripping with jewels, to stretch their legs and have something to eat and drink.

The war had changed all that, and the highwaymen were out of business. No one dared to be ostentatious now. Dressing up in fine clothes had always been frowned upon by Puritans, and they'd made sure it was associated with the king and his 'Catholic' ways. It didn't seem to matter that there were plenty of seriously rich Roundheads, or that some so-called Puritans had flamboyant tastes. And nobody considered the many Royalists who came from very poor backgrounds. People were afraid and, in public at least, everybody dressed in ordinary clothes and tried to look anonymous.

The crowd that had gathered outside the inn that afternoon was typical of this. It was made up of many sorts of people, both rich and poor, but they all looked the same and were there for the same reason. They had come to see their king, and even the presence of poker-faced Roundhead soldiers couldn't dull their excitement.

They cheered when the children and Mignonne arrived, but then groaned with disappointment when the royal party was led straight to the door of the inn.

Mignonne was trotting happily beside Elizabeth when she heard a bird caw somewhere overhead. She stepped away from the door and looked up. Sioluc was perched on the guttering. Her body was tipped slightly forward, and her diamond anklet was glinting in the sunshine.

She chattered throatily at Mignonne, who was just about to bark 'hello' when a pigeon swept close beside her. Remembering what had happened with the gull at Exeter, Mignonne squealed and ducked under Elizabeth's skirt, but the pigeon merely swerved away and landed on a nearby tree.

Mignonne followed the children into the inn and along a passageway to a parlour. It was a pokey room with low ceilings and tiny, mullioned windows. The walls were clad in wooden panelling, and the floor was of rough stone. Everything was dark and gloomy and there was a strong odour of tobacco smoke and ale mixed with boiled cabbage. Mignonne had never seen or smelled anything quite like it.

Elizabeth said in a very shrill voice that she hadn't known such places even existed, which made Mignonne cringe with embarrassment. But then James laughed and said he'd stayed in far worse whilst he'd been away fighting, and he thought the parlour rather fine. That made everyone feel better, especially the inn-keeper.

A young man brought cordial for the children and a bowl of water for Mignonne. They all drank thirstily, and the children had just drained their glasses when, hearing a roar from the crowd ouside, they rushed over to one of the windows and pressed their noses against the glass.

The king had arrived and was waving and smiling and having to urge his horse forward as people pressed to see him. All around him, men were cheering and throwing their hats in the air, and women and children were tossing posies of flowers and herbs. A man shouted, 'Long live the king!' and everyone else joined in, 'Long live the king! Long live the king!' whilst the Roundhead soldiers stood stock still with their lips pursed and their faces set like stone.

King Charles left his horse and made his way into the

parlour, where James and Elizabeth were so excited to see him they nearly knocked him over. Henry, on the other hand, stood in the corner looking pale and shy. As James had pointed out, he'd been a baby when he'd last seen his father, and had no idea who this strange man was.

The king found a seat wide enough for them all to share, and pulled Henry onto his knee. The little boy went very still.

'Do you know me, child?' the king asked gently.

'No, Sir,' came the reply.

'Then let me tell you...'

Whilst the king introduced himself to his son, the young man who'd brought the drinks came into the room again. He bowed, and the king nodded graciously and pointed to Mignonne.

Thinking that somehow the nurse and the guards from St. James's had caught up with her, Mignonne shot under a settle and pressed herself hard up against the parlour wall. When the young man knelt on the floor and peered at her, she curled her upper lip and tried to look fierce.

'What ails you, man?' the king asked. 'Take her firmly. She will not bite.'

'The pox I won't,' thought Mignonne.

Elizabeth had been so absorbed in seeing her father again that she hadn't noticed Mignonne's plight. Now she removed the king's arm from around her waist and stood up.

'Please, papa,' she said. 'Do not have her sent home.

She wanted so very much to see you.'

The king laughed and ruffled his daughter's hair.

'Sweetheart,' he said. 'Did I ever send your mother's dog away from me without good cause? No. Nor would I. She is simply going to the stables to sup. She will be returned to us soon. You have my word on that.'

On hearing this promise, Mignonne crept out from under the settle and allowed the young man to pick her up and carry her out of the room.

At the rear of the inn was a courtyard where visiting coaches could be given small repairs and washed down before their onward journeys. Three sides of this yard had low buildings, some of which were set aside for storing coaches and keeping spare wheels, parts and harnesses. The remainder of the buildings were stables.

As she crossed the courtyard, Mignonne recognised her own coachman. He was sitting amongst a circle of ostlers and stableboys, and was drinking ale and wolfing down a hunk of salted meat. Mignonne barked at him, and he raised his tankard and smiled.

The young man carried Mignonne under an archway, the entrance to a stable block. A bowl of warm stew was already waiting on the herringbone red-brick floor, and Mignonne was set down beside it.

'Eat up,' said the young man. 'I'll come back for you when you've finished.'

CHAPTER TWENTY-FOUR

Mignonne wasn't interested in eating. She wanted to see the stables. She walked around the bowl without touching its contents and wandered up the stalls.

Most of them were empty.

The coaching business was in dire straits, and many of the country's horses had been commandeered for war. Mignonne wondered how many of them had died since the one whose muzzle she'd stepped over so nonchalantly at Edgehill. She heard a clop of hoof on brick, and looked up. A horse had moved forward from the rear of its stall and was arching its neck towards her. Mignonne nodded, and the horse nodded in reply.

Another head, dappled grey and with a deep brown forelock, was several boxes further on. Mignonne recognised it as the king's mount, and raced up to it. She stood on her hind legs and touched its nose with her own. The horse whickered, and Mignonne continued on her way. She passed the six bays who'd brought her here, and then a row of empty stalls until, at the very end of the block, she smelled sweat and dry mud, and heard the swishing of a tail and the sound of tack being removed. She stopped and glanced at the other horses for reassurance. Their heads were silhouetted against the light from the stables' arched entrance, turned towards her and watching curiously.

The door to the stall creaked open, and the whites of a pair of eyes flashed, low down in the darkness.

Mignonne raised her nose towards them.

Dog.

She lowered her upper body and wagged her tail to show she was willing to be friends, and something shifted to her left. Not the dog or the horse, but a man. He leant over the door of the stall and balanced a trooper's saddle on its top edge.

'Hello, pretty,' he said.

He hooked a bridle over the door's bolt and led his horse out of the stall on a rope.

'Stay, Blackie,' he said gruffly.

The dog's eyes flashed again, and Mignonne shrank away from the sight of the trooper's scarlet wool coat. He was one of Oliver Cromwell's men.

He pushed the door half-way shut, and began to lead his horse towards the sunlit archway.

'Come pretty,' he coaxed. 'Let's find a quiet place.'

Mignonne wasn't sure who he was talking to, but she followed him, all the same. She wanted her stew.

'I saw you arrive with the king's brats,' the trooper continued conversationally. 'You must be hungry. Let's see if we can't find a tit-bit for you, shall we?'

He paused and leered over his shoulder.

'Heh, heh,' he cackled. His few teeth were black with rot.

When Mignonne heard a creak of hinges, she glanced back and saw that Blackie the dog had left his stall and was now skulking behind her. The trooper walked on. Most of the horses moved to the back of their boxes as he passed, but the king's mount kicked its door and squealed.

Outside, the afternoon sunshine was dazzlingly bright.

Mignonne blinked and the trooper snapped his heels together.

'Commander Cromwell!' he barked.

Mignonne trembled as a long shadow fell across her path. She looked up and saw a tall, lumbering fellow standing over her. His vast body had blocked out the sun, leaving his face in darkness.

'So this is the queen's poodle,' he mused in a gravelly voice.

Mignonne tried to shrink away, but Cromwell was already kneeling down. She could see his face now. It was rough and heavy, with leathery, warty skin and an alarmingly large nose.

Her eyes darted sideways, searching for rescue. They settled on her coachman and his ostler friends. Their conversation had stopped. All eyes were turned in her direction.

'Prince Rupert had a poodle too,' Cromwell said as he took her paw in his hand. 'Its name was Boy. They say it was bewitched, and held Rupert in its thrall. And that when it died, the prince's powers died with it.'

Mignonne swallowed.

'Do you have special powers?' Cromwell asked her gently. 'Are you bewitched?'

Mignonne shuffled sideways and saw her coachman put down his tankard.

'If she *is* bewitched,' the trooper said, 'and let's say she met with a small but fatal accident...'

He rubbed his hands together gleefully.

'What are you suggesting?' Cromwell spat, his voice suddenly gruff.

'That the king's powers, or what remains of them, might die with her. Just like Prince Rupert's did,' the trooper replied.

'Except that this is the queen's dog, not the king's,' said Cromwell.

'We could tie her legs together and bind her to a table...'

'Whatever for?'

'That's how to tell a witch. You starve them, then watch them day and night to see if the Devil's imps come visit. They always confess, in the end.'

Mignonne saw the hint of a smile in Cromwell's face. She tried to snatch her paw back, but he cupped his other hand over it.

'Somehow I don't think that applies to dogs,' he said reassuringly.

Just then, Mignonne heard a soft paw tread behind her, caught the scent of coarse, doggy hair and felt hot breath on her neck.

'Don't let that trooper touch you,' Blackie growled over her shoulder.

'Hey!' Mignonne's coachman called. 'Leave that poodle be!'

Cromwell let go of Mignonne's paw and turned towards the shout.

'The man is right,' he told the trooper. 'You must not mess with this dog. That is an order.'

The trooper sighed.

'Yes, Sir,' he said, and he began to lead his horse away.

Mignonne turned to face Blackie.

He was a handsome lurcher, not black at all, but sandy-coloured.

'What did he mean, "mess with me"?' she asked him.

Blackie stretched out his front legs and lowered himself to Mignonne's height.

'I was a Royalist dog too,' he answered. 'Still am, at heart, but I was captured at Naseby.'

He tipped his head forwards.

There were two pink scars where his ears had once been.

'They were hacked off to make me a Roundhead,' he said.

Mignonne's first reaction was to recoil in disgust, but when she saw the sadness in Blackie's eyes she reached out a paw and carefully stroked his scars.

'I'm sorry,' she whispered. 'So sorry.'

'Run!' barked the lurcher. 'Run lest they change their minds.'

Mignonne fled.

She hadn't been back in the parlour very long when the king rang the service bell three times, and the young man appeared yet again.

This time he was carrying Cavendish.

Mignonne was so pleased to see her friend that she completely forgot to tell him about her run-in with the trooper.

She and Cavendish leapt about boisterously for several minutes and everyone else had to wait for them to calm down. Only then could Elizabeth smother Cavendish with kisses whilst James picked him up and introduced him to Henry. The little prince didn't remember the spaniel any better than he had its master, but he happily patted Cavendish's broad head and shook the silky paw that was offered to him.

Soon they were all curled up together, with the dogs lying across the king's lap and the children clinging to his arms and laughing at the funny stories he told. When the innkeeper came to announce that dinner was served, they sighed, untangled themselves, and traipsed along the passageway to another room.

This was larger and brighter than the first, and someone had taken a lot of trouble to make it welcoming. The polished oak table had been decorated with nosegays and candles and laid with jugs of wine, and there were dishes of hearty stew and plates of fruit and cheese.

Everyone took their places and the children were

allowed a little wine, and, what with this, the heat from the candles and the joy at seeing their father again, their cheeks were soon flushed pink whilst their eyes sparkled.

Towards the end of the meal, Mignonne and Cavendish heard a heavy footfall in the passageway outside.

'Why can't he leave us alone?' Cavendish growled as he jumped protectively onto the king's lap.

'Who?' Mignonne asked.

'Oliver Cromwell.'

'Oh, I forgot to tell you...' Mignonne began.

'Ssshht!' Cavendish snapped.

There was a knock at the door.

'Enter!' the king called.

The door opened partway, Cavendish curled his upper lip and Prince James rose to his feet. Elizabeth and Henry went on chattering, completely oblivious to the sudden change in mood, until James reached instinctively for his sword.

Elizabeth stopped mid-sentence.

'Wha...?' she gasped.

'Sit down, James,' said the king calmly.

But James's hand had already dropped impotently to his side. He was no longer an armed soldier. He was a captive prisoner and could carry no weapons. He thumped his fist on the table in frustration, the door swung wider, and Cavendish growled again.

There was complete silence whilst all eyes turned to Oliver Cromwell. He was as huge as Mignonne remembered, especially by comparison to the king. His clothes, which Mignonne had been too terrified to notice earlier, were plain and traditional. He wore a buff leather tunic with a pointed white collar and cuffs, suede breeches and thigh high leather boots. All of these were slightly grubby and very well worn. The cloth was thinning and frayed, the buff was tired and patchy, and the boots were cracked at the ankles, down at the heels and scuffed at the toes.

Cromwell didn't venture any further into the room, but stood in its doorway with his body bowed and his hands clasped behind his back.

It was the king who broke the spell.

'You'll take wine, Sir?' he asked.

'Don't you dare,' Cavendish snarled.

'By your favour, no, Sire,' came Cromwell's welcome reply. 'You must rather be with your children. And...I...I must...'

The man the king and his family feared, who held His Majesty prisoner, and who was famous throughout the land for his political speeches seemed completely lost for words.

'...must take some air. Sire...I...'

'Off you go, then,' muttered Cavendish. 'Good riddance.'

CHAPTER TWENTY-FIVE
Bo's House.
The 21st Century

'Oliver Cromwell,' Cavendish spat. 'Everybody said he would become His Majesty's most dangerous enemy. How right they were! I blame Cromwell, and Cromwell alone, for what happened next.'

'What did happen next?' Bo asked meekly.

She could see that Cavendish was furious.

'Not long after our visit to Maidenhead,' he began, 'Cromwell moved my master and me to Hampton Court Palace. We were still prisoners of course, but we had small pleasures. The king played tennis and went hunting, and Mignonne and the children were allowed to visit us. Then the king heard a rumour that someone might try to murder him. On the afternoon of 11th November 1647, he and I retired to our room. The king's excuse was that he had some urgent letters to write, but he didn't so much as pick up a quill. The room had two doors and he locked one from the inside and took me through the other. It led to a back staircase and a secret, underground tunnel.'

'No! Where did the tunnel go?'

'To the river. Horsemen were waiting for us there.

Ugh. I hated riding. We galloped through the night to the south coast. It made me feel thoroughly sick, I can tell you. Then, as if *that* wasn't enough, I had to get into a *boat!*'

'Oh, I can sympathise with that,' said Bo. 'Mignonne would have enjoyed the riding bit. She liked horses. But a boat? No.'

'We didn't go far, fortunately. Just to the Isle of Wight. We ended up at a place called Carisbrooke Castle.'

Bo shivered.

'I went to a castle once. It gave me the creeps.'

'Well this one wouldn't,' Cavendish said defensively. 'Not then, anyway. We hadn't escaped, as such. We were still prisoners, but the king felt safer and we were very comfortable. We had each other and some of our servants, and familiar things like the king's books and pieces of his own furniture. He even had his coach sent down from London. And there was plenty to do. We still went hunting and hawking, and they built a bowling green on the lawn, specially for us. The only thing the king wasn't supposed to do was write secret letters.'

'Which he did, of course,' said Bo.

'Of course,' said Cavendish. 'He had to keep trying to get help and support. The letters were smuggled out by his laundress, Mrs Wheeler. She was a very talented smuggler.'

'Carisbrooke doesn't sound at all bad,' said Bo. 'I wonder if...'

'No,' said Cavendish flatly. 'Mignonne never went there. She was very close to Elizabeth by then, and the king would never have parted them. Elizabeth would have been very upset. I know that because I was missing Mignonne myself.'

'You said the king had his coach sent down to the island,' Bo persisted. 'Perhaps I could stow away.'

'It never happened,' Cavendish replied. 'You can't do things that never happened. Lesson four, remember? History cannot be changed.'

'Oh, well,' Bo sighed. 'That's that, I suppose.'

Cavendish gave her a sideways glance.

'It's not?' asked Bo hopefully.

The spaniel nodded distractedly and raised a paw.

'Hush,' he said. 'Give me a moment.'

Bo sat obediently whilst Cavendish's ears twitched and a dimple of concentration appeared on his forehead.

'It might be possible,' he finally said.

He paused, clearly still working things out.

'It might just be possible,' he repeated. 'Mignonne never went to Carisbrooke, but you might be able to get there another way. You'd have to become something which *did* go there.'

'*Thing*? What do you mean, *thing*? I don't want to be a *thing*, Cavendish. Can't I be you?'

'No, obviously.'

'Well what then? Give me a clue! What sort of thing? What could I be? What was there? Please don't say a table.'

'A table won't do,' Cavendish replied. 'It has to be something living. A mouse, perhaps. Or a rat. A cockroach, beetle, spider, woodlouse, silverfish, ear-wig, moth...? Take your choice.'

'Forget it. I don't want to be any of those.'

'It's not a beauty contest.'

'It's not how they *look*,' said Bo, fibbing a bit. 'It's what they *do*. All that scuttling. And, well *you* know, *stuff*. I want to be something nice.'

'You seem to be missing the point.'

'But if I'm a mouse or a rat...'

'I shan't chase you. The place was over-run with them. I gave up after a few days. A cockroach might not be such a good thing, though. The guards used to stamp them to death with their boots.'

Bo winced.

'What about a bird? I'd rather be a bird. There must have been birds. Maybe Sioluc was there.'

Cavendish raised an eyebrow.

'What makes you say that?' he asked.

'Um. I don't know. It seems possible. She was clever. She could fly. We know she was a Royalist. She turned up in Oxford and Exeter, she might even have been at Dover, so why not the Isle of Wight, too? Where *is* the Isle of Wight, anyway?'

'Off the coast of Portsmouth,' Cavendish replied. 'And, yes,' he added grudgingly, 'Sioluc was there.'

'See!'

'We don't even know if you can do this, Bo. There's no guarantee you'll get to Carisbrooke. You'll just have to concentrate and see what happens.'

'This is ridiculous,' said Bo in frustration.

'Clear your mind,' Cavendish soothed, 'and look

above you.'

Bo raised her eyes to the coal hole's skylight.

'Now. You need to find something of this moment. Ideally, it should be a bird. Can you see any birds?'

'Yes. There's a pigeon...'

'Best not.'

'Oh, right. On the tree, then,' offered Bo. 'The crow on the tree?'

'Much better,' Cavendish said. 'Perfect, in fact. Have a good look at it. Do you see how black it is? How strong its legs and beak are?'

'Yes,' Bo replied. 'Strong and black, like Sioluc.'

'Now close your eyes,' Cavendish whispered.

'Just a sec',' I need to clarify something.'

'What's that?'

'If I'm a cockroach, which, by the way, I have no intention of being...'

'And you get stamped on? That'll be it.'

'It?'

'The end of it. Oh, I see what you mean. No. *You'll* be fine. I'll be able to bring you back here.'

'But I'll never see Carisbrooke?'

'Other than some dodgy plumbing and the underside of a guard's boot? No. Now close your eyes.'

'Wait!' Bo barked.

'What now?'

'Is the room going to spin?'

'I've no idea. Do you want to do this or not?'

'I...I'm not sure.'

'I think you do. Now imagine the king. It is evening.

He is sitting by a fire, reading. He has his cane in one hand. You remember his cane, the one with the silver top?'

Bo nodded.

'The room is wood panelled. It has a four-poster bed,' Cavendish continued, 'and a great many books and papers. You are Sioluc...you land on the king's window and...close your eyes, Bo...'

It was like being suspended in the centre of a room-sized tumbler dryer. There was nothing beneath her feet and nothing to hold onto. Yet she herself felt steady, even as everything spun around her in a blur.

The walls of the dryer were covered with scores of pictures. They had narrow white frames, like old photographs, and were butted together as though someone had stuck them there to make a vast collage. But they weren't photographs at all, because their subjects were moving, and every one of them was an animal, or part of an animal.

Bo recognised some of these creatures, but there were many she didn't.

A sea anemone pulsated its tentacles. A monkey chattered and grimaced, showing sharp yellow teeth. Snow flurries whipped against a huddled group of penguins, and zebra tails flicked flies on a dusty plain.

The spinning slowed and the animals became more familiar.

Bo saw a pair of squirrel paws rolling a hazelnut, the watchful eye of a rabbit, and a ladybird sunning its wings, but there was no sign of Sioluc, nor any other bird. Not even a blue-tit.

Slower still, and there were fewer pictures, but they were larger and more detailed.

These were the things that Cavendish had said were at Carisbrooke.

Bo barked at the fat, furry body of a moth and the armoured back and rippling legs of a woodlouse. She started as a cockroach waved its brown feelers and scuttled towards her, and she shivered when a rat dragged its scaly tail across her line of sight. She gagged at the wriggling ear-wigs and the slithering silverfish, and almost died at the sight of eight, high-stepping spider's legs.

Mice, rats, cockroaches, beetles, spiders, woodlice, silverfish, ear-wigs, moths; all passed before her eyes.

Still no Sioluc, and Bo began to panic. She wondered how she'd get out of this nightmarish place. She thought about lying down, but she was afraid to move her feet. They were still rock steady, in spite of the spinning, and she didn't want to upset things by shifting her weight.

Soon a new set of pictures appeared. There were only twelve of them, and the spinning almost stopped as they slotted into an even block and then began to ripple outwards like water in a pond. The ripples receded, the spinning stopped with a shudder, and the pictures merged into a single image.

Bo's heart skipped a beat and she pranced backwards. Standing in front of her was a raven. She glanced at its feet but they were buried in long grass. There was no way to see if the bird was wearing an ankle bracelet.

Bo took a step forward. She stretched her neck and tried to touch the raven with her nose. There was a sharp tap and, rather than soft, warm, forgiving feathers, she felt hard, resistant glassiness. She hadn't touched the bird at all. She'd banged her nose on a mirror. No, not her nose, something else. She crossed her eyes and peered along her snout. It had transformed itself into a massive bill, dense and strong and the colour of iron. She tipped her head to the left, and her right eye stared back at her, black as coal with heavy, blue-grey lids. She glanced at her chest and saw that her matt black curls had turned sleek and shiny. Her normally fluffy, pompommed tail was pointed and feathered, and her four woolly legs had become two scaly ones, standing in long grass. She raised her right foot, and gasped. It was huge, with gnarled toes, fearsome, flesh-tearing talons and a delicate diamond ankle bracelet.

She leant forward and gently touched the bracelet with the tip of her beak. Then she brushed her foot backwards and forwards over her breast feathers until the diamonds twinkled.

Finally, she opened her wings, and flew.

CHAPTER TWENTY-SIX
Carisbrooke Castle, The Isle of Wight, England.
December 1647

She landed on the rim of a gutter, opened her wings again, and jumped. She swooped, and felt the wind course through her plumage as she rolled in the air and dived among the treetops.

She swept over the castle's roof and past its flickering windows, then stretched out her legs and landed. She lifted her wings one at a time and preened them.

Finally, she darted to the king's window.

His Majesty was wearing a long woollen dressing-gown and was sitting beside a fire, reading. Next to him, on a small table, was a glass of wine and a plate of fruit and cheese.

He held his book in his left hand, and his cane in his right. His fingers toyed with the cane's silver top, and his ruby ring caught the light in dancing pink sparks.

Sioluc cocked her head and laid one eye against the window so as to see the rest of the room.

Much of it was taken up with a huge four-postered bed. It was draped with tapestries and silken tassels,

and there was a stack of pillows bordered with deep lace at its head. The same lace trimmed the king's sheets, which had been folded down over a velvet quilt. In the centre of this quilt was a bearskin rug, and in the centre of *that*, curled up and fast asleep, was Cavendish.

Surrounding the bed, on shelves and tables, on a writing desk, and even on the floor, were piles of books and papers. There were quills and inkwells, candles and snuffers, and all sorts of boxes. The largest of these were made from leather decorated with studwork, but there were others of ebony and fruitwood, and some were embroidered with birds and flowers.

Sioluc thought it a very cosy little room for a king and his dog, but it looked lonely, all the same.

She tapped her beak against the window, and the king glanced up.

She tapped again.

Cavendish jumped from the bed and the king put down his book and, leaning heavily on his cane, gathered some cheese in his free hand. Then he came to the window and pushed it open.

'Well, bird! Not yet abed?' he asked.

He held out the cheese in the flat of his palm and she took it as gently as she could.

'I would you have sweet dreams on such a supper, bird.'

She nodded at him, arched her neck to remove a speckle of cheese from her breast feathers, and stretched her right wing. She was feeling sleepy.

The king took a step back and bowed.

'Welcome,' he said. 'Come.'

He looked down at Cavendish, who was now sitting on the floor beside him.

'Come,' he said again. 'My dog means no harm. His name is Cavendish. Come, bird. Share our little home. 'Tis warmer than a raven's nest, I'll vouch. And better guarded too.'

She hopped into the room and glided towards the king's chair, and he closed the window behind her.

The king remarked on her diamond bracelet and laughed. Then he took up his book again, and she and Cavendish settled beside the hearth and dozed. When he heard the guards push their beds against the far side of the door, the king blew out all but one of his candles, which he carried to the side of the bed and set down on a small table. He knelt to say his prayers, took off his dressing-gown, snuffed out the candle, and climbed under the covers. Soon he was fast asleep with Cavendish snoring at his feet and Sioluc roosting, head under one wing, on the canopy above.

Sioluc stayed close to the king and Cavendish for all of the following day. She pranced beside them as they strolled about the grounds, and flew into the Great Hall and perched among its rafters to watch them dine. Later, she followed them back to their room, where she sat on the king's desk or the arm of his chair whilst he wrote his letters. Some of these were composed of perfectly normal words, but others were a series of apparently random numbers, and seemed to make no sense at all.

After several hours of writing in his meticulous, elegant hand, the king leant back in his chair and sighed.

'There,' he said. 'All done. What's needed now is a visit from Mrs Wheeler.'

Right on cue, there was a knock at the door and a plump, ruddy-faced woman came into the room. She was dressed in a heavily gathered skirt with a woollen bodice, and was balancing a large wicker basket on one hip. Her long, silver hair was plaited, twisted into a bun, and held low on the nape of her neck by two tortoiseshell combs and a brown felt hat.

She bobbed a curtsey.

'Evenin', Sire,' she said with a swift glance at Sioluc. 'Is that bird botherin' you? Shall I get someone up to shoo it away?'

'No, no. It makes a pleasing companion. But you might open the window. It *is* somewhat airless in here.'

'Certainly,' said Mrs Wheeler.

She set her basket down beside Cavendish, who was sprawled on the bed, then bustled across the room and pushed the window ajar.

'Now then, Sire,' she said as she returned to her basket. 'I've brought you clean shirts and two fresh nightgowns. And you'll find there are nine *kerchiefs* too.'

She removed a pile of freshly laundered clothes from the basket and pulled away a corner of its cotton lining. Hidden behind the lining were nine fat little squares of folded paper. She withdrew these carefully and handed them silently to the king.

He nodded, slipped them into one of his boxes, and picked up one of his newly written letters.

'I would you take this,' he said, 'and do wash it well, for I find it *Smales*.'

Sioluc bobbed excitedly at the mention of her friend, then watched anxiously as the king folded the letter over and over until it was as small as he could make it.

'And here are two *shirts*,' he added, giving the same treatment to two more letters.

He passed all three to Mrs Wheeler, who had just slipped them down the side of her basket when Sioluc heard a noise. She flew from her perch and landed beside the door, then tipped her head and listened.

'And this is my favourite lace collar...' said the king as he picked up one final letter, kissed it, and began to fold it up, '...which I would have you *scent* with lavender of *France*,' he added.

He had almost finished his folding when Cavendish heard something too, and jumped down from the bed.

Someone knocked on the door and, momentarily distracted, the king dropped the letter.

Sioluc hopped backwards, and the king bent to retrieve the letter. He had it between his thumb and forefinger when the door opened, and a man stepped into the room. It was Colonel Hammond, Governor of the Isle of Wight, and the man whose job it was to keep the king locked up.

'Colonel Hammond,' said the king.

'Sire,' the colonel bowed his head, 'and Mrs Wheeler.'

He nodded at the laundress and she curtsied back.

'I hope I am not disturbing you,' Hammond said courteously.

'Not at all,' the king replied.

The letter was still in his hand. He couldn't be sure whether Hammond had spotted it or not. He turned slightly, and tried to push the letter up his sleeve, but Hammond took a step towards him.

'I'll take that,' he said.

'What, Sir?' the king asked innocently.

'The paper.'

'Oh, this? This is just...'

Ravens are not designed to fly from a standing start. If they cannot launch themselves from a height, they must have room to run, stretch their massive wings and gather power. Yet somehow, even in that confined space, Sioluc managed to leap far enough into the air to snatch hold of the letter with her beak. Only when she had it safely in her grasp did she raise her wings, beat them once, and dart through the open window.

'...just a scrap,' ended the king.

'The bird brought it in,' said Mrs Wheeler.

'Yes,' the king added, 'you know how they like to collect things.'

'Indeed,' Hammond said.

'May I enquire as to the purpose of your visit, Sir?' asked the king.

'It was merely to suggest an evening stroll,' Hammond answered as he wandered over to the window, 'but I see now that it is beginning to snow.'

He put his head through the window, looked from side to side, then withdrew and pulled the window shut.

'Ah,' said the king. 'It is too inclement, then. Perhaps tomorrow?'

'Tomorrow will do very well indeed,' Hammond bowed. 'Good day to you, Sire.'

'Good day,' replied the king.

Mrs Wheeler and the king said nothing to each other until Hammond's footsteps had faded away. 'That was close, Sire,' said Mrs Wheeler eventually.

Her face had gone quite pink and she was fanning her chest with one hand.

'Aye,' the king agreed.

He held a finger to his lips and pointed to the window.

Mrs Wheeler nodded, tip-toed across the room and quietly opened the window again. There was a moment's pause, the king and his laundress held their breath, and then Sioluc glided back into the room and dropped the king's letter onto his desk.

The king sat down heavily on his chair and exhaled, then picked up the letter and examined it.

It was slightly damp but still so tightly folded that the ink hadn't run at all.

He kissed it again, and passed it to Mrs Wheeler.

'As I was saying,' he smiled, 'I would have you *scent*

this with lavender of *France*.'

'Certainly, Sire,' said Mrs Wheeler as she slipped the letter into her basket and folded back the lining. 'You were right about that bird then, Sire. A most pleasing companion she makes, what with her clever ways. And such a pretty little anklet she has! I never saw the like!'

'Nor I,' said the king. 'She is curious in every sense, is she not? I hope she stays with me and does not fly away. I like to fancy she is an angel in disguise.'

'I do hope so, Sire.'

Mrs Wheeler hitched the basket onto her hip and went to where the king had piled his dirty washing on the floor. She collected a nightgown, two shirts and a lace collar, dropped them into her basket, and bobbed another curtsey.

'G'night, Sire,' she said with a broad grin.

'Good night, Mrs. Wheeler,' the king replied. 'And godspeed, for I am anxious for more...er... *kerchiefs*.'

'Yes, Sire. I'll do my best, Sire,' Mrs Wheeler giggled.

And she left the room, closing the door behind her.

CHAPTER TWENTY-SEVEN
Bo's House.
The 21st Century

'So?' Cavendish asked.

'Sioluc!' Bo squealed. 'I was Sioluc! I know it was her because I was wearing the diamond bracelet.'

'Tell me. Start from the beginning.'

'Well. I saw the things you'd mentioned. The cockroaches and things. They were moving about in pictures and spinning past me. Then they turned into a sort of mirror but instead of seeing my own reflection, I saw a bird. I raised my right leg, and there was the bracelet! Next thing I knew, I was flying! It was evening and I was at Carisbrooke Castle. I did rolls in the air and things and then I swooped over the roof and landed outside the king's window. You were asleep on the bed.'

Bo continued her story, and was halfway through telling Cavendish about Colonel Hammond and the dropped letter when she tailed off and peered suspiciously at her friend.

'You don't seem very excited,' she said. 'Did you *know* I'd be Sioluc?'

'I had a pretty good idea.'

'Then what was all that stuff about cockroaches and things?'

'I had to prepare you Bo,' Cavendish replied. 'I *wanted* you to be Sioluc, but I could have been wrong. You have an extraordinary gift but it can be contrary sometimes. You *could* have been a cockroach or a silverfish. You could have been anything, but there were many connections between Sioluc and Mignonne.'

'Mignonne said from the start that Sioluc seemed familiar,' Bo agreed. 'She even wondered if Sioluc was the raven she'd seen at Dover, but I don't think she was. I think that was another raven.'

'Me, too. I don't think Sioluc came onto the scene until later. When there was all that business at Exeter, and afterwards.'

'When Mignonne had the strange dreams? I know. I'd wondered about that too. It was as though she'd had a bird's eye view of the queen's journey to Falmouth.'

'Well our suspicions were right,' said Cavendish. 'Mignonne and Sioluc were individual animals of different species. They lived at the same time, they were both Royalists at the heart of the king's camp. Yet their lives did more than merely cross. They were soul sisters, Bo. Do you understand what that means?'

Bo shook her head.

'It means that you were just as much Sioluc as you were Mignonne. For me to suspect that is one thing, but for you to *prove* it is something else entirely. There is no way you could have known about that incident with Colonel Hammond and the letter unless you'd been there in person. What you have done is very rare, Bo. *Very* rare. And now you must keep in touch with your Sioluc side. You must be her as often as you can.'

Bo looked worried.

'What's the matter?' Cavendish asked.

'Are you saying I can't be Mignonne anymore?'

'No. I'm not saying that. Mignonne is important. Mignonne is *you*. I'm only saying that Sioluc gives you other options, other things to see, a different view of things. As Sioluc, you can go where Mignonne never went.'

'And vice-versa?'

'Of course, vice-versa. That's the beauty of it all.'

'Oh good,' said Bo, 'because I'd like to visit Elizabeth, James and Henry again. I have a feeling that they played a very important game, that Mignonne was there, and that it had something to do with hiding.'

'By Jove, you're right!' Cavendish exclaimed. 'It was a very important game indeed.'

'I *knew* it,' Bo replied. 'Isn't that odd? I've remembered something about Mignonne's life before I've even got there.'

'Not odd at all,' said Cavendish. 'I told you things would get easier with practice.'

CHAPTER TWENTY-EIGHT
St James's Palace.
26th April 1648

Mignonne and the children had a new game, which they called 'hide and seek.'

It had been James's idea, and he'd made sure they played it every evening before supper.

The children were still under house arrest, so at first the guards had trailed whoever was hiding, which gave the game away immediately and made it all a bit pointless. But James had persevered and, after a couple of weeks, the guards had grown used to his ritual. Now they hardly bothered to watch it, and James and Mignonne had become 'hide and seek' champions.

Henry may have been small and able to squeeze himself into the tightest spaces, which made him potentially good at hiding, but he was still very young, and had a tendency to leap out and squeal with excitement when anyone came close.

Elizabeth was far too sweet-natured for the game. She hated to fool people, and always owned up before she was found, which was admirable but useless.

Mignonne, on the other hand, could not only crawl

into nooks and crannies which even Henry couldn't reach but also had an advantage when it came to finding people. She could track them by scent, though even she could sometimes take ages to find James. His experience as a soldier had made him competitive and ingenious, and he seemed able to vanish at will.

That evening, they all traipsed into the garden as usual and, as was also usual, Edmund Smales went with them.

He was still pretending to be a Roundhead, still acting out his West Country footman persona. It was a brilliant bluff, and Parliament had no idea that he was a double agent and one of the king's most trusted servants.

Several pairs of guards were patrolling the grounds, and the white-haired gardener, Mr Sowerbutts, was tinkering with the fruit trees on the west wall. Mignonne made a beeline for the old man, and he delved into the pocket of his leather apron and retrieved one of his soily biscuits.

Just then, though, Smales called Mignonne back. The hide and seek was about to begin. Mignonne snatched the biscuit and scampered across the lawns with it. Most of it crumbled away as she ran, so she paused to swallow the rest, and promised herself she'd go back to Mr Sowerbutts as soon as she could.

The rules of the game stated that, since Henry was the youngest, he must always be first to hide, so off he went whilst the others closed their eyes and began to count to a hundred.

Mignonne was still counting, eyes tight shut, when Edmund Smales suddenly grabbed her by her topaz collar and dragged her back inside the palace, across the hall and down a corridor. There he opened a cupboard and produced a piece of dried venison.

'Look, Mignonne,' he said.

He waved the meat in front of her nose.

It smelled delicious.

He shot his hand out towards the cupboard.

Mignonne went after it.

Smales dropped the venison, whisked his hand away and slammed the cupboard door.

'Pox!' Mignonne muttered in the darkness. 'I can't believe I fell for that!'

She listened to Smales's retreating footsteps and wondered why he'd done such a thing, and why he was walking away from the garden instead of back into it. She concluded that James had added a new twist to the game but forgotten to tell her about it. No matter. She would sit in the dark, chew her venison, and wait patiently for someone to come and find her.

When she realised no one was even looking, she began to bark.

Still no one came.

She stretched out a paw and prodded the cupboard door.

It remained firmly shut.

She banged against it with her nose.

'Owp!' she yelped.

She moved as far back into the cupboard as she could,

took a deep breath, and flung herself forward with all her might. The door flew open with a crack and a crash, and Mignonne was catapulted across the corridor.

She picked herself up, had a good shake, and looked about. No one had seen her.

'Good,' she thought, 'because that was *slightly* embarrassing.'

She was trotting nonchalantly back through the hall when she spotted Elizabeth and Henry walking very fast in the direction of the children's salon. Elizabeth was holding her little brother tightly by one hand, and was leaning over him with her forefinger pressed against her lips.

Mignonne ducked under one of the hall chairs. She thought it would be fairer and more fun if she counted to ten before going to find the children, but she'd only got as far as 'seven' when she saw Edmund Smales again. He had a bundle under one arm, and was hurrying towards a tradesman's entrance which led onto a lane at the side of the palace. Mignonne decided to follow him. She waited until he'd gone through the tradesman's door, then trotted up to inspect it.

'Perfect,' she whispered.

In the days before the war, she'd often used this door to go for secret walks. She knew that if it wasn't pulled properly shut she could open it by herself. Smales had left the door just as she liked it.

She pressed her nose against the jamb and rotated her head, slowly prizing the door ajar until there was just enough room for her to slide her paw behind it. That done, she gave it another quick shove with her nose, and ran through the gap.

It was beginning to rain by then, so Mignonne stayed in the shelter of the doorway and watched Edmund Smales from a distance.

He'd gone south along the lane and was now under the big oak tree which grew opposite the garden gate. He was kneeling on the ground, untying his bundle. He pulled away the strings that bound it and pushed them into his pocket, then stood up and shook it open.

It was a lady's dress and shawl.

'How very peculiar,' thought Mignonne.

She wanted to know what on earth Smales was up to, but there was something so furtive in his manner that she didn't think it wise to show herself, and anyway she didn't want to get wet.

By the time she reached the hall again, the April shower had passed over, and sunlight was flooding through the doorway to the garden. There was no sign of James, and she was bored with looking for Elizabeth and Henry, so she settled for Sowerbutts and his biscuits instead, and set off in the direction of the fruit trees. When she reached the west wall, though, there was no sign of the old gardener.

'What is going *on* here?' she muttered to herself. 'Where *is* everybody?'

She was almost directly opposite the oak tree and could see its top branches. She realised that if only she could get higher she'd be able peek over the wall and see what Smales was doing.

She gazed up at some plum trees.

They were still pretty bare, with only a few spring leaves. If she was ever going to learn how to climb a tree, now was the perfect time of year. On the other hand, she'd never considered climbing a tree, whatever the state of its foliage. In her opinion, tree-climbing was an extremely silly exercise and strictly for cats.

She sighed resignedly.

'I see I must make an exception to my rule,' she decided.

She stood well back and chose a sturdy-looking specimen with a fork between two low boughs. Then she took a deep breath and braced herself. She put all of her weight onto her hind legs, and sprang.

Much to her amazement, she managed to make it onto the fork in one leap. From there she picked the strongest-looking bough and edged along it. At the point where it divided into two branches, she chose the thickest, straddled it, and heaved herself along and up, until she could see over the top of the wall.

There was no sign of Smales.

'Rats! Where's he gone *now*?' she snorted.

At that very moment, she spotted James.

He was directly beneath her, glancing nervously over his shoulder, and crouching so low he was almost crawling.

Mignonne had completely forgotten about the game of hide and seek. Now she decided to wait quietly in the tree until James had selected a hiding place. Then she'd climb down, somehow or other, and 'find' him.

She leant as far out of the tree as she dared and kept an eye on James whilst he weaved in and out of the fruit trees. Finally, he reached the garden gate on the west wall. Then he stood upright, took one last look behind him, and disappeared onto the lane.

'That's cheating,' Mignonne growled. 'He knows we're not allowed out there. It's *dangerous*.'

But her objection was half-hearted.

Now she *really* wanted to find out what was going on.

'Has James gone to meet Smales?' she wondered. 'Or is that a coincidence? And what's with the dress?'

She was about to take another peek over the wall when she heard a rustle of undergrowth. She glanced to her left and saw that Sowerbutts was emerging from a clump of ferns near the gate.

She looked over the wall.

Smales had reappeared. He was standing under the oak tree with James and another man, someone Mignonne had never seen before. The two of them were helping James into the lady's dress.

Mignonne bent to where she'd last seen Sowerbutts. She wanted to know if he was watching James's antics too, but the gardener had disappeared again. Then, somewhere behind her, she heard running footsteps. She turned her head gingerly and craned her neck.

Sowerbutts was rushing across the lawn, waving a hoe in the air.

He wasn't shouting. In fact he was remarkably quiet until he found the guards. *Then* he said something. Mignonne couldn't hear what it was, but she could see him point towards the garden gate.

He was telling the guards that James had gone onto the lane.

Mignonne whipped her head back towards the oak tree. James was in the dress now, and was wrapping the shawl around his head.

Mignonne barked.

Smales frowned, stepped out from under the tree and looked to left and right.

Mignonne heard the guards running towards the gate.

She barked again, and Smales raised his head at last, caught sight of her up a plum tree, and opened his mouth aghast. Then he cupped a hand over one ear and listened.

Mignonne didn't wait to see if Smales had realised what was happening. She just hurled herself out of the tree, landed heavily with a walloping thud, rolled, found her feet, and raced for the gate.

She reached it at the same time as the guards and, when they flung it open, she darted between their legs.

The lane was deserted.

Mignonne galloped over to the oak tree and circled it, then looked up. The guards were cussing and shouting and running up and down the lane like headless chickens with Sowerbutts trailing after them wheezily. None of them were watching to see what Mignonne did.

She sighed in disbelief and lowered her nose to the ground where she swiftly picked up the scent of Prince James and Smales. The other man's scent was there, too, and after following it for only a short distance, Mignonne realised that he and James had gone down the lane together.

Smales had not been with them.

Mignonne shook her head bemusedly, then turned and hurried back through the garden gate to the palace. When she reached the children's salon she found Edmund Smales calmly reading a story to Elizabeth and Henry.

That evening, after the two children had gone to bed, Smales came to find Mignonne and sit beside her.

'James has escaped,' he said.

'Yes,' Mignonne mumbled, 'I'd rather gathered that.'

'You were supposed to stay in the cupboard until it was all over,' Smales laughed affectionately. 'We've been planning this for a long time, Mignonne. We couldn't allow it to go wrong at the last minute. We thought that if you saw James go through the gate you might bark. That would have alerted the guards. Hence the cupboard. But we had not reckoned on your determination. Nor on the treachery of Sowerbutts. Thank goodness you *did* bark, Mignonne. You saved the day.'

Mignonne licked a paw and wiped it over her face. She was trying to appear blasé, as though rescuing princes from the brink of disaster was something she did all the time. In reality her heart was thumping with

175

pride and delayed terror. She still couldn't believe she'd climbed a tree.

'Sowerbutts eh?' Smales added quietly. 'Who'd have thought it? Ratting on Prince James like that? Still, there's no harm done. Sowerbutts gave *himself* away, and that's a good thing. I can keep an eye on him, now. Better yet, he doesn't know about me. The Roundheads still think I am one of them, and Prince James is safe. That's the main thing. He looked very fine dressed up as a lady, don't you think? My friend will take him to the boat and then, God willing, he will make it to the continent and see his mama at last. You remember her, don't you, Mignonne? She is your mistress, and she will hear how clever you've been.'

CHAPTER TWENTY-NINE
Bo's House.
The 21st Century

'That was the frightening thing about those times,' said Cavendish wistfully. 'Even an old gardener with silver hair and a pocketful of dog biscuits could turn out to be a spy.'

'I'm pleased James got away,' Bo answered, swallowing hard. 'I really am. The queen, Prince Charles, Prince James, Prince Rupert, even baby Hetty-Anne have all escaped. So Elizabeth and Henry must be next, and the king, too. They are all alone now, you see. So they must be next.'

Cavendish changed the subject.

'Why don't you see if you can be Sioluc again?' he suggested. 'Take another trip to Carisbrooke.'

CHAPTER THIRTY
The Isle of Wight.
28th May 1648

The tide was rising, and miniature white-topped waves were rippling shoreward. Several boats were bobbing on the water, and a few gulls were sitting on the pilings and crying out to each other across the creek. Apart from them, though, all was quiet, and Sioluc saw no people.

She turned in the sky and flew inland and directly southwest, towards Carisbrooke Castle.

She stayed low and kept her eyes peeled until, just east of the castle, she spotted some movement amongst the trees. She swooped and came in to land on a dry-stone wall at the side of a quarry. She was within a few paces of the men she'd been seeking.

They were huddled together in hushed and earnest conversation. Three of them were still on horseback, but the other two had dismounted and tied their horses, and a spare one, to some scrappy trees.

Sioluc bobbed up and down in approval, then took off again, heading for the castle.

The king had been moved to a new, much smaller

and more secure room, all thanks to his many escape attempts. His efforts had come to nothing, of course, other than to make his life more miserable. He was watched much more closely, his quarters were cramped and basic, and many of his comforts and loyal servants, including Mrs Wheeler the laundress, had been removed.

This new room was one of the highest in the castle, and had a perilous drop beneath it. Even so, a special wooden platform had been fixed to the wall below, and guards stood there day and night, just to make doubly sure that the king didn't try to get away.

As Sioluc swept past the platform, she noticed that the guards were feeding a gull with scraps of bread. The bird caught sight of her, too, and squawked aggressively. She ignored it and continued her flight up the steep incline to the king's open window. There she settled on its sill and looked back at the gull. It had returned to its food and was pecking contentedly.

Sioluc rubbed her diamond ankle bracelet over her chest feathers and hopped through the window.

The king was sitting in his fireside chair. He was still surrounded by his books, papers, inkwells, quills and boxes, but they seemed to overwhelm him now, crammed as they were into this tiny room. There had been no space for the great tapestried and four-postered bed, and the one he'd been given instead was a poor substitute. But it did have a simple frame with curtains along it, and tasselled ropes to draw them open and closed. He still had the crisp white lace, the quilt and the bearskin rug, and he still had Cavendish, curled up in the middle of it all, fast asleep.

Sioluc flew across the room and landed on the arm of the king's chair. He stretched out a hand and cupped it gently over her head. He had grown very frail. Worry, loneliness and a lack of sunshine and fresh air had turned his skin pale, and his hair was thin and grey. He seemed much older than he really was.

'Well, bird,' he said. 'The day is here at last, and all is in place. I cannot let these good men down. I must at least attempt to carry out their plan. But I do say that part of me is loathe to leave.'

He nodded in the direction of the bed.

'How can I take him?' the king whispered under his breath. 'Yet how will I manage without him? Or he without me?'

Sioluc glanced at Cavendish. The last few months had taken their toll on him too, and he was even frailer than his master. Even so, there was no way that the king could carry him down the castle's steep walls. He would need every ounce of his failing strength to make his own escape. But to separate the king and his dog now, after all they'd been through together? Sioluc didn't consider it an option.

'There must be a way,' she thought as her black eyes darted round the room. 'There *must* be! We *have* to find a way to get Cavendish out of here.'

Then she had an idea.

She jumped from the king's chair and hopped across

the floor.

Since Mrs Wheeler's departure, a new system had been set up to deal with the king's laundry. The wicker basket had been discarded, and the king now piled his dirty clothes onto a square of linen with a leather handle at each corner. The smoothness of the linen meant the delicate fabrics weren't snagged, but also made the hiding of letters impossible.

Every morning, a guard returned the cleaned items and then gathered the handles of the used square in one hand to form a makeshift sack. He heaved this onto his shoulder to carry it away and dropped a replacement square by the door, ready for the next load of royal washing.

The soiled laundry had already been collected for that day, and the only thing on the new square was a lace collar. Sioluc picked this up in her beak and flung it sideways.

'Hey bird!' the king chided. ''Tis only a collar. Why quarrel with it thus?'

Sioluc stepped onto the square and pranced about. She flew to the bed and bounced up and down beside Cavendish. She flew back to the linen and pranced, onto the bed and bounced. She did this six or seven times, chattering all the while, until the king put down his reading and turned to watch. He was laughing by then but, though Sioluc was pleased to see him amused, she had something far more urgent in mind.

She just didn't know how to explain it, and time was running short.

In desperation, she caught hold of one of the leather handles with her beak, hopped backwards, and dropped it in the middle of the square. Then she picked up a second handle and laid it beside the first. Just as she was reaching for a third, the king rose from his chair.

'I see at last!' he exclaimed. ''Tis strong enough, I'll vouch.'

He bent down, swept an arm through all four handles, and lifted the linen off the ground.

'Now we have need of a rope,' he said.

He looked around the room.

'Some type of rope,' he muttered to himself. 'Something which will reach from the window to the guards' platform.'

Suddenly he laughed again, scooped up the linen and rushed to the bed. He laid the linen down, smoothed it out and then gently lifted Cavendish and placed him in its centre. Reaching up, he pulled the curtain ropes from their rings, knotted them together and threaded them through the leather handles. Then he clenched the ropes in one hand and hoisted Cavendish clean into the air.

The dog looked momentarily baffled and then went back to sleep.

The king lowered him down and tucked the bearskin snugly around him, then rubbed his hands in glee and danced around the room. Having found a way to include his beloved companion, he could now happily concentrate on the last stage of his plan to escape.

He took a kid glove from a drawer in his desk and removed a small phial from one of his boxes.

'I have it on good authority that this will work,' he said, pulling the glove over one hand and heading for the window with the phial. 'Aqua fortis, they call it. 'Tis fearsome stuff, bird.'

Sioluc had spent many an evening watching the king laboriously filing away at the back of the metal bars on his window. She had even helped him by flapping her wings or cawing to muffle the sound of his sawing. The results were impressive. The bars still appeared intact from the front, but their backs had been whittled so far down that they were holding together by barely a thread.

'Stand back now,' said the king.

He removed the phial's stopper and carefully dribbled its contents over the bars.

There was a hiss and a fizz and a puff of poisonous fumes, and the bars' last remnants dissolved clean away.

'Did you see?' the king chuckled delightedly. 'Marvellous stuff! Would I had a barrelful. I might make Mr Cromwell disappear! But hush, bird. Did you hear a noise below?'

She had.

The guards on the platform should have been quiet as mice in those last few minutes. Their bribes had been paid long ago. All they had to do now was help the king and his spaniel to the ground. After that it would be up to the men whom the raven had seen by the quarry. Their mission was to come through the woods to the castle, collect the escapees, and take them to the waiting horses. From there they would all ride to the creek, where one of the anonymous little boats would catch the turning tide and take the king out to the Solent, and thence across the English Channel to safety.

The king and the raven leant from their newly barless window and looked down at the guards' platform. There were more guards there than ever before, and every one of them was bristling with weapons and staring up at the window.

Sioluc slipped from the sill and flew silently up the north wall and over the roof of the castle.

From a gutter overlooking the courtyard, she watched the rest of the castle's guards gather quietly and load their muskets. It seemed the game was up. The king's hope of escape had been dashed, but at least he was safe. His friends, on the other hand, were in grave danger. They would be waiting in the woods by now, unaware that a search party was setting out to hunt them down.

Sioluc thought about trying to find them first. But then what? Any warning she gave might be heard by the guards too, and that could do more harm than good. It was long after dusk, and no bird, other than owls and nightingales, was likely to call unless disturbed. The guards would probably run straight to the noise, and then the men would have no chance.

It was at that moment that Sioluc remembered the gull she'd seen pecking at bread on the platform.

'He must have been a passing visitor,' she told herself as she left the gutter. 'Otherwise he'd have found the king's friends by now and be making a racket to alert the guards.'

She recalled the warning that she and every other raven had received from their anointed leader, Corex. When the war had first begun he'd sent his message to every corner of the country.

'Beware the grey birds,' he'd said. 'Their allegiance is worthless and often brief. For if the tide of fortune turns, they'll turn with it, and fly the other way.'

'Grey birds,' Sioluc tutted as she flew back past the platform. 'When it comes to a contest, grey birds have always been fickle. They'll sit on the fence until they spot a likely winner. Only *then* will they take sides, yet if their choice is proven wrong they'll flit again.'

She reached the king's room and found him sitting resignedly by the fire, reading a book. He knew it was all over. The curtain ropes had been neatly coiled, Cavendish had been moved back to his bearskin, and the linen square was lying by the door with the lace collar in its centre.

Some time later there was a knock at the door, and Colonel Hammond entered the room. Hammond was a Parliamentarian, but he had Royalist connections and liked the king as a person. He was sorry the king hadn't behaved better, instead of constantly trying to smuggle letters and escape. Without all that, Hammond wouldn't have been compelled to remove so many of his privileges. It certainly wasn't something he'd enjoyed, and he'd often wished that the thankless task of keeping the king prisoner hadn't fallen to him.

'Well, Sir?' the king inquired as Hammond strode towards him.

'I am come to take my leave, Sire,' Hammond replied with a wry smile. 'For I hear you are going away.'

He went on to explain that the guards who'd been bribed to stay quiet had panicked instead, and raised the alarm. He added that none of the king's friends had been caught, and the search for them had been called off.

Even so, when Hammond left the room, he and the king both knew there would be no more escape attempts.

The king retired early that night and, as she'd done on every night for the past six months, Sioluc settled herself on the canopy above his bed.

But rather than falling asleep with her head under her wing, she stayed wide awake and listened anxiously for Cavendish's every breath.

When morning came, the king didn't get up, but sent a message to ask if Colonel Hammond would be so kind as to come to his room.

The Colonel arrived, heard Cavendish's ragged wheezing, and ordered silence in the castle. He then fetched a dish of water, placed it on the king's bedside table and tip-toed discretely away.

In London, Mignonne woke with a start and suddenly remembered Cavendish as she'd last seen him. He'd been sitting on the king's knee at Hampton Court Palace with his head in a bowl of soup.

Mignonne smiled to herself and pushed her nose deeper into Elizabeth's pillow.

Meanwhile, Sioluc gathered droplets of the water into her beak and tried to make Cavendish drink.

He opened his eyes, but turned his head away from the water and shuffled deeper into the warmth of his master's arms.

Then everyone held their breath as, with a last, contented sigh, Cavendish died.

CHAPTER THIRTY-ONE
Bo's House.
The 21st Century

Bo flopped onto her side.

'I don't think I can take much more of this,' she told Cavendish despairingly. 'Sioluc just watched you die. Now the king has nothing. No one.'

'He has Sioluc,' Cavendish said quietly. 'She continued to visit him.'

'Well I won't go back again. Not to Carisbrooke. Not ever. I couldn't bear to see the king sitting there all on his own.'

'Then why don't you go to the trial?' Cavendish suggested.

'Trial? Whose trial?'

'The king's trial,' the spaniel replied.

'The king was on trial? For what?'

'Anything they could think of. Treason. Treachery. Warmongering.'

Cavendish lay down and put his head between his paws.

'My poor master had to endure days of it,' he sighed. 'It happened at Westminster. It was January, and very cold.'

'But Mignonne didn't go to that, surely?' asked Bo incredulously.

'Not Mignonne, no,' Cavendish replied. 'Sioluc.'

CHAPTER THIRTY-TWO
St. James's Palace.
27th January 1649

Sioluc had spent more than a year with the king, most of it on the Isle of Wight. Then, last November, he'd been moved from the island and she'd followed him to Hurst Castle, a grim, wind-torn fortress on the Solent, and then, briefly, to Windsor Castle.

Now they were both in London again, and Sioluc was pleased to be home, though very *displeased* about the reason for it. King Charles was being tried for treason and as a tyrant who had brought war on his own people.

The raven lifted her right ankle and polished her diamonds absentmindedly. Then she hopped across the snow-covered roof of St James's Palace and took to the skies.

She flew northeast to the village of Charing, where she clipped a bend in the River Thames and settled herself midstream, heading due east towards the city of London. To her left and right, wide open spaces soon condensed into built-up areas of closely packed houses, neglected, filthy streets and rambling alleyways.

She reached the river's only bridge, London Bridge,

swooped over the roofs of its crammed shops, and swerved north. She passed quickly over the bridge's gates and their dozens of poles stuck out at odd angles. Each one was topped with a rotting human head, supposedly that of a traitor. These days that meant the Royalists, and even the king himself, if his enemies could have their way.

A few hundred yards more, and she reached The Tower of London. She skimmed the river's slow waters and opened her beak to gather a drink. Then she folded her wings and darted through Traitor's Gate and over the roofless remains of the Great Hall.

Four ravens stood chattering on the battlements of The White Tower.

She landed beside them and they fell silent, bowed, and brushed their cheeks along the ground.

'Corex!' she demanded.

'Straightway,' cawed the largest bird.

He disappeared through a gap in the tower's stonework and re-emerged within seconds.

'Corex will see you immediately,' he said.

Sioluc hopped across the roof and squeezed through the gap.

Beyond it was a gently sloping shaft which opened into a space between the tower's vast walls. The original purpose of this space was long forgotten, if it had ever had one, but by 1649 it had been the headquarters of British ravens for several hundred years.

It was also the official residence of their anointed leader.

That leader was always addressed as Corex.

Sioluc landed in the little room and bowed to a distinguished, elderly bird with silvered plumage.

He was sitting on a bed of fresh hay which had been gathered that morning by the junior ravens. They had cleaned it scrupulously, stem by stem, before flying it to the den in a daily, centuries-old ritual.

All around him was his collection of treasures. It lay about the floor, hung down from the ceiling joists and was stuffed into the stonework's many nooks and crannies. There were strips of satin and silk and silver lace. There were buckles, buttons, brooches and coins, and fragments of jewellery and broken glass. Many of these items were very old and some were extremely valuable, but all had two things in common; they all sparkled, and they had all been searched out by individual birds and carried to the den as presents.

Any bird who visited Corex was expected to bring him a shiny present.

Sioluc, in her rush, had forgotten that.

'Forgive me,' she said, bowing again. 'I am empty-beaked.'

Corex cocked his head and fixed her with one of his beady black eyes.

'Granted,' he said.

He lowered his bill.

'I cannot,' he added shakily. 'I cannot recall a more terrible day.'

'Aye, Sire,' Sioluc replied. 'And these days past have been terrible enough. That farce at Westminster! They

call it a trial? Pah! Any MP who was against it has been excluded from the Commons! By doing that, the king's enemies made sure to diminish his chances of acquittal, and...'

Sioluc's tirade was interrupted by a scuttling on the roof above, and a young, sleek raven skated down the shaft and plopped into the den.

He shook himself and bowed.

'Good morning, General,' said Corex. 'No present from you either, I see. Still. We have more important things on our minds, do we not?'

General tipped his head and glanced at Sioluc.

'Go on,' she said encouragingly.

'Sioluc and I have been watching the trial,' General began in a hesitant voice, 'and well, I thought...I wanted to make a suggestion.'

'What's that?' Corex asked.

'Well, Sire,' General stammered.

'What he means to ask you,' Sioluc intervened, 'is whether, this being the last day of the trial, we might not, let's say *influence* the proceedings?'

'Lord knows I've considered it,' replied Corex. 'We could cause havoc in the chamber. We could even waylay a Parliamentarian or two. But we would only *postpone* the verdict, and that would prolong His Majesty's anguish. No. There is nothing we can do. We must let the verdict come.'

He hesitated a moment.

'It may be hard for you, Sioluc,' he said gently. 'You've grown fond of His Majesty. If things should go against him...'

Sioluc bowed.

'Sire,' she said.

'Go quickly then,' Corex added hurriedly. 'And take your places.'

Sioluc and General turned to leave.

'Sioluc?' Corex cawed.

'Yes, Sire?'

'You are a very good Royal Ambassador. One of the best. We must hope they do not put you out of a job today.'

Sioluc and General left the tower together and flew along The Strand and then south. Within minutes they were approaching the Palace of Westminster and its great, six hundred-year-old hall.

'We must stay away from the roof!' General called. 'They've put marksmen there lest anyone tries to rescue the king.'

'They won't shoot ravens!' Sioluc called back.

'You've been away from London too long,' General replied. 'These days, who knows what they'd do?

The two birds banked the steep face of the palace and headed straight for its magnificent stained-glass window. Amongst the hundreds of pieces of coloured glass which made up its design was a tiny gap where one had fallen out. Feeling with their feet, the birds landed on the gap's lower leads and squeezed between them, into the hall. Then they darted beneath its ancient, hammer-beamed ceiling and settled themselves on their favourite perch, a carved angel. From there they looked down at the gathering below.

And what a strange gathering it was.

King Charles was sitting in a wooden dock. The fabulous, pearl-encrusted Star of the Order of the Garter sparkled on his shoulder, but other than that he was dressed entirely in black. His black velvet cloak, black hat, black breeches and black shoes accentuated the whiteness of his skin and the greyness of his hair. He looked old, frail, and utterly exhausted.

In front of him was a tier of wooden benches built four or five high. This was where the judges sat, including Oliver Cromwell, who was in the very back row. These judges were also dressed in black, with the notable exception of John Bradshaw, the President of the Court, who had added a bullet-proof hat and a cloak of scarlet.

Sioluc knew, as did everyone, that the judges, Bradshaw in particular, had been carefully selected. It hadn't been easy. Even some of the most ardent Roundheads, people who'd opposed the king for years, had refused to play a part in this farce. They knew the trial was wrong. Also absent were many people who'd supported the king and could have helped him. They didn't want to be a part of the trial either, but nor were they prepared to speak up and do something to stop it.

Sioluc glanced at the galleries where the wealthy people sat, all got up in their fancy finery as if they'd come to watch a play or hear a recital of music. It *seemed* frivolous and shallow, but Sioluc was pleased to see their rustling silks and glittering jewels. At least *someone* was showing fortitude.

She turned on her perch and studied the far end of the hall and the members of the public who were standing there. They were muffled up in winter clothes of woolly blacks and browns, dark hats and knitted shawls, and were packed tightly together and held in check by a double row of Roundhead soldiers. Somehow, some of the more intrepid amongst them had managed to escape these soldiers and their raised muskets, and had scaled the walls for a better view. Now they were clinging precariously to the window recesses.

A tiny pink sparkle caught Sioluc's eye, and she tipped her body forward and turned her head sideways. Immediately below her, the king's fingers were fiddling with the silver top of his cane, and his delicious ruby ring was glinting in the cold January light. Sioluc sighed miserably and fluffed up her feathers.

Bradshaw rose to his feet and coughed.

'He's about to deliver the verdict,' whispered General.

'Now, therefore,' Bradshaw began importantly, 'upon serious and mature deliberation...'

'Well that's a lie, for a start,' said General under his breath.

'Ssshht, listen!' Sioluc scolded.

Bradshaw rambled on.

'This court is fully satisfied in their judgments and consciences that he hath been and is guilty of the wicked designs and endeavours in the said charge set forth...for all which treasons and crimes this court doth adjudge that he, the said Charles Stuart, as a tyrant, traitor, murderer, and public enemy to the good people of this nation...'

Bradshaw paused dramatically and everybody held their breath.

'Shall be put to death by the severing of his head from his body!'

The crowd gasped as one, and Sioluc's legs crumpled.

Cromwell and about half the other judges were rising to their feet.

'Aye! Aye!' they cheered.

Sioluc lost her grip on the angel and tumbled sideways. For an instant she didn't really care that she was dropping like a stone towards the hard floor nearly a hundred feet below. Then, just as her instinct for survival kicked in, she felt General swoop beside her to break her fall and bear her up. She mustered all her strength and beat her giant wings until she was on the rise again. When she reached the safety of the angel, she looked down at the judges' benches.

Cromwell and his friends were still on their feet, but those who had wanted to save the king were slumped in their seats.

They had lost by one vote.

The king had not spoken throughout the trial, and had

refused to answer any questions.

Now he shouted.

'Will you hear me a word, Sir?' he asked.

'You are not to be heard after sentence,' Bradshaw replied coldly.

'No, Sir?'

'No, Sir, by your favour, Sir.'

The king leant heavily on his cane, and tried to stand up.

'I m...m...may speak after the s...s...sentence,' he stammered. 'By your favour, Sir, I m...may speak after the s...s...sentence. By your favour, hold! The sentence, Sir. I say, Sir, I do.'

Bradshaw ignored him and turned to the guards.

'Withdraw your prisoner,' he said.

General and Sioluc left their perch on the carved angel, flew out of the hall and settled on a balcony. From there they watched the king being carried back to St James's Palace in a litter. Roundhead soldiers escorted him, the streets were deserted and it was eerily silent.

'Nobody did anything,' said Sioluc miserably. 'No one stood up for him.'

'They would have lost their lives, most like,' General replied.

CHAPTER THIRTY-THREE
St James's Palace.
Later that day

Mignonne and the two children entered the king's apartments together, but Princess Elizabeth was first to reach him. She rushed ahead of the others and threw herself into his arms. She was crying so hard she couldn't breathe, and kept making heart-rending gulping noises.

Mignonne could hardly bear it, but she knew she mustn't interfere, and anyway Prince Henry had her firmly by the collar. All she could do was stand quietly by and watch.

The king grasped Elizabeth's upper arms to hold her straight. He begged her to stop crying and listen to him. What he had to say was very important, he added, and she must try to concentrate and remember it.

Elizabeth took a deep breath.

'Yes, papa,' she sobbed.

The king wiped away her tears with his thumbs and told her how good and brave she was. Then he sat down and pulled her close to him and said that he loved her and that it was his wish that she, and her brothers and sisters, should forgive his enemies.

'You will be sure to let your brothers and sisters know this?' he asked.

Elizabeth nodded, and the king gave her a message for her mother, Queen Henrietta Maria.

'Tell her that I never stopped thinking about her,' he said. 'Tell her that I will love her forever.'

Poor Elizabeth began to sob again, and the king stroked her hair.

'Sweetheart,' he pleaded. 'You will forget what I am saying.'

Elizabeth replied that she really wouldn't, and that she would write it all down as soon as she could.

'Then sit here beside me,' her father replied, 'whilst I talk to Henry.'

He beckoned to the little boy, who let go of Mignonne's collar and climbed onto his father's lap.

'They will cut off my head,' said the king, 'and perhaps make you the king. But mark what I say. You must not be made a king whilst Prince Charles and Prince James still live, for they will cut off their heads, should they catch them. And then perhaps they will cut off yours too, and therefore I charge you, do not be made a king by them.'

Henry said solemnly that he'd rather be torn in two.

The king called Mignonne to his side, and ruffled the fur on the top of her head.

'You must remember what I have said this day,' he repeated. 'You must remember and try to stay together.'

He hugged both children, took each of their faces in his hands, and bent to kiss their foreheads. Then, quite suddenly, he asked them to leave. He got up, leant on his cane, and crossed the room without looking back. At the door to his bedchamber, he hesitated. He turned to face the children, opened his arms wide and ran unsteadily towards them for one last hug. Then he turned again and walked away. This time he went inside his bedchamber and closed the door behind him.

Mignonne and the children were driven to their new home, Syon House, where Elizabeth asked for a fresh sheet of paper, a quill and some ink.

'I must write down the important messages papa has given me,' she told Mignonne. 'You will help me, will you not?'

When the writing materials arrived, Elizabeth lifted Mignonne onto her knee and smoothed the paper. Then she dipped the quill into the ink and, in her very best hand, began:

'What the king said to me, Jan 27 1649, being the last time I had the happiness to see him...'

CHAPTER THIRTY-FOUR
Bishopsgate Street, London.
29 January 1649

Sioluc settled on the roof of The Green Dragon tavern in Bishopsgate Street and shook out her feathers. She eased her head between her shoulder blades, fluffed herself up against the sharp wind, and began to think about Edmund Smales.

She'd first got to know him at Exeter. Then, after the queen's escape, he'd lain low for a while, and Sioluc had dropped in on him from time to time at his hiding place, an isolated cottage in the Oxfordshire countryside. Eventually, though, Smales had returned to London and become a regular at The Green Dragon, where Sioluc had taken to joining him.

She cawed contentedly at the memory of those nights. She'd become such a regular herself that the tavern owner and his wife had begun to keep a bowl of scraps under the counter, specially for her.

But Sioluc's promotion to Ambassador To The King had

meant leaving London for Carisbrooke and losing touch with Smales. Sioluc loved her job, but she'd missed Smales. It was over a year since she'd last seen him, and though she was back in London now, the king's trial had kept her too busy to look for her friend during the day. And so, every evening for the past week, she'd come to The Green Dragon in the hope of finding him.

Before her first visit, she'd wondered if the place was still open. So many shops and businesses had closed down. People were poorer now than they'd ever been before the war. Sioluc had watched them shuffle sadly through the streets and clutch at their thin clothes. She'd seen how they tried to avoid eye contact with the crippled soldiers who sat huddled in doorways begging for a crust.

She'd flown towards the tavern hesitantly, that first time. She'd been afraid of discovering it was boarded up, but when she'd heard raucous singing from the end of the street and then smelled tobacco and ale, she'd known that the tavern had survived. She'd darted through its partially open doors and discovered with relief that nothing had changed.

The building's low rooms had been as noisy and as thick with smoke as ever. Men had still been sitting around on benches and leaning across rough tables with their tankards in front of them. Some had had wooden plates, trenchers they called them, with hunks of bread and mouldy-looking cheese to pick at, but most had been there to drink.

Sioluc had made straight for the counter where the

taverner's wife had raised her hands in surprise.

'Look, Jack!' she'd exclaimed to her husband. ''Tis that bird again! The one with the bracelet!'

'We thought we'd lost you,' she'd told Sioluc. 'Now then, let's see what we might 'ave for your fancy. Not much, I fear.'

She'd wiped her hands on her apron and called across the room to a serving wench.

'Bella!' she'd hollered. 'Scrape off any crumbs you find! Our bird is back!'

Bella had laughed and set about her task with gusto, and Sioluc had soon been sitting on the counter with a trencherful of scraps.

When she'd returned the next evening, her old bowl had been back in place, and the scraps had been ready and waiting for her. She'd been back six nights in a row since then, but Edmund Smales had never appeared.

It was beginning to snow.

Sioluc left the roof of The Green Dragon, swept through the tavern door, and landed on the counter.

She peered sideways into her bowl.

It contained a veritable feast of cheese rind, apple cores and salt pork. Even Corex didn't always eat this well, nowadays. Soon she was so absorbed in her meal that she didn't notice Edmund Smales enter the tavern.

He approached her from behind and stroked her back.

Instinctively, she leapt in the air and gaped her beak.

'Sorry, bird. I see I did scare you,' said Smales in his

fake accent. 'It's good to 'ave you back. Where you bin, then?'

'We thought we'd lost 'er, didn't we?' the taverner's wife remarked. 'What'll it be for you, Mr Smales? Mornin' Dew?'

Smales nodded.

'Three pots,' he replied.

When the drinks arrived, Sioluc flew onto Smales's shoulder and he carried her and the pots of ale to a small table in the darkest corner of the room. Two people were already there, but it seemed they'd only just arrived. One of them was propping a walking stick against the wall, and both had a fine dusting of snow on their pulled down hats and tightly wrapped cloaks. They sat close together with their backs to the door, and it wasn't until Smales had squeezed himself around the table and into the space opposite them that Sioluc realised who they were.

She hopped across the table and tipped her head to see them better. Even in the shadow of his hat, Prince Charles's face was stunningly handsome. He was eighteen years old and had the dark complexion, hair and eyes of his quarter-Italian, quarter-French blood. And the Danish part of him had given him extraordinary height. Sioluc reckoned he was well over two yards in stature, which made him nearly a foot taller than his own father, the king.

Richard Cheevely was slightly older than Charles and almost the complete opposite in looks. What Sioluc could see of his hair was dark, for sure, but he was still light of skin and small in build, and he still had those remarkable grey eyes.

'It is all arranged,' Smales whispered in his natural voice. 'I'll take you to the horses, then you must ride to Blackfriars and the alehouse they call The Drover's Cart.'

'I knows it,' said Cheevely.

'Good,' Smales nodded. 'A boatman named Cripps will meet you there and take you downriver to a merchant ship. It is scheduled to sail for the continent at dawn. Be on it.'

'Yes, Sir,' Cheevely tipped his hat.

'Is there really no chance?' asked Prince Charles.

'No,' said Smales. 'Absolutely not. If they were to catch you...if your father were to hear of it...how do you think he would feel? Don't you think he has enough to worry him?'

The prince sighed.

'You're right,' he said remorsefully. 'It was a bad idea from the start. I just wanted to see him.'

'It was the worst possible idea,' said Smales.

He stretched out a hand and laid it on Prince Charles's arm.

'Had I been able to find a way,' he added gently, 'you know I would have done so. But His Majesty is too well-guarded. They would catch you for sure and send you the same way as him. Now drink your ale,' he urged, 'and I'll see you to the horses.'

When the two young men had drained their pots, Prince Charles reached for his cane and stood up slowly with his back hunched. He hadn't been in London for years, and very few people would recognise him, but he was wise not to draw attention himself. Men with sticks or crutches were of less note these days than someone of Charles's uncommon height.

Sioluc flew onto Smales's shoulder and she and the three men quietly left The Green Dragon and stepped into the snowy street. In an alleyway leading off it, a gaggle of urchins was minding two horses.

Smales paid the boys and shooed them away.

'Won't you ride with us to Blackfriars?' Prince Charles asked plaintively. 'We can share a saddle.'

Smales shook his head.

'No,' he said. 'I have an appointment to keep. Cripps will be looking out for you. Now go.'

He hugged the prince and slapped him on the back, then took Cheevely's hand and pressed it between his own.

'Godspeed,' he said as the young men mounted their horses and trotted away. 'Godspeed.'

Smales stood in the snow with Sioluc on his shoulder and watched them go.

'I wonder, bird,' he said, as the horses rounded a bend in the street and disappeared from view. 'I wonder when we will see them next.'

He sighed.

'Godspeed,' he whispered again.

He crooked a finger and stroked Sioluc's throat absentmindedly.

'Perhaps I should have gone with them to The

Drover's Cart. But no. Meeting them at all was risk enough. My face is too well-known in these parts, and the king's enemies still believe I work for them. If one of them had happened upon me and stopped to say a few words, if they had recognised the prince...'

Smales shivered and began to walk southwards.

'He came to see his father, you know. It was madness, of course. He was lucky to have Cheevely. It seems they've kept in touch these past few years. Cheevely got a message to me at St. James's, but there was nothing I could do to grant the prince's wish.'

When Smales reached the end of Bishopsgate Street, Sioluc spread her wings.

'Off again?' said Smales. 'Well then, so must I. Good night, bird.'

Sioluc cawed a reply and leapt from Smales's shoulder.

She reached the Drover's Cart within minutes, and took a perch on its chimney stack. She could see the man Cripps standing under an overhanging doorway. He had been a Thames boatman all his adult life, and was well known to the ravens as an honest fellow and an ardent supporter of the king. Sioluc nodded approvingly. Smales had made a good choice.

She heard the horses before she saw them. They were approaching the alehouse, walking slowly. She crossed to the far side of the roof and looked down. The horses had stopped by then, and Cheevely and Prince Charles were leaning out of their saddles and discussing something in earnest. Their voices were low, hardly more than whispers, and too distant and muffled by snow and river fog for Sioluc to make out what they were saying. Finally, they seemed to reach a conclusion. They nodded to each other, and Cheevely laughed. Then they turned their horses and trotted away.

Sioluc followed at a safe distance until she was certain that the two young men had no intention of making their rendezvous with Cripps. Then she cried for help, hoping that another raven would hear her plea and track the horses whilst she went to find Smales. But it was useless. She gave up and let the prince and Cheevely go.

She flew straight to the Tower of London. She knew that Corex would probably be roosting, and that to wake the old bird unnecessarily was a punishable offence, but she considered this an emergency. She only hoped he'd agree.

The birds guarding the entrance to the shaft on the roof of The White Tower were fluffed up against the weather and their backs were turned when Sioluc swooped down beside them. But they were quick enough off the mark to block the path to Corex's den until they saw who the visitor was. They noted her grim expression, hopped aside and cawed urgently.
'News! News! News!'
Sioluc slid down the shaft and landed in the den,

where Corex was very far from being asleep.

'Sioluc,' he greeted her.

'Sire,' she bowed. 'You were not roosting?'

'Roosting?' the old bird retorted. 'No. I have not roosted these past few days. But you were not to know that, and you would not trouble me for a trifle. What has happened?'

Sioluc told Corex about her visits to The Green Dragon to find Smales and how he'd finally appeared that evening, along with none other than Prince Charles and Richard Cheevely. She described the two young men, the arrangements Smales had made for their escape and the instructions he'd given them. Finally, she related how Smales had led them to the horses and said his good byes.

'He told them he couldn't accompany them to The Drover's Cart,' she added. 'He said he had an appointment. So I went there myself. I saw Cripps waiting for them, but as they neared the alehouse they paused and had a discussion. Then they turned and rode away.'

'You followed them,' said Corex. It was not a question.

'Only until I was sure they wouldn't be meeting with Cripps, Sire. Then I came here.'

'What are they up to?' Corex cawed.

'I don't know,' Sioluc replied. 'I *do* know that the prince wanted to see his father.'

'Which he cannot do,' Corex pondered.

'Cripps kept his appointment,' Sioluc added, 'but the prince and Cheevely didn't. There is no way they can get to the merchant ship now.'

'Then they will still be here tomorrow,' said Corex.

'You don't think they'd do anything foolish, do you?'

'I hope not. For now I'm more worried about their enemies, and what *they* might do, should they find them.'

Corex raised his head.

'Swithin!' he screeched.

In a flash, one of the raven guards shot down from the roof and into the den.

Corex didn't look up.

'It is time for the nightingales,' he said grimly.

Swithin bowed and scrambled back up the shaft.

'Go to your roost now, Sioluc,' Corex ordered. 'We can do nothing more tonight. The nightingales will alert our kin, and patrols will be mustered by dawn. They will have the descriptions you gave me. We will find the prince, and Cheevely.'

CHAPTER THIRTY-FIVE
The Banqueting House, The Palace of Whitehall.
30th January 1649

Despite the snow, people had been gathering since first light. Now the streets around Whitehall were thronging with those who'd failed to secure a place in the small, cordoned off area in front of The Banqueting House.

There, jutting out from one of the building's elegant first floor windows, and barely a few feet above the heads of the tightly packed crowd, was a hastily erected wooden platform, a scaffold.

Sioluc and General landed on its top rail and looked down.

'They're very crushed,' noted General.

'The space is well-chosen,' Sioluc added.

She nodded at the Roundhead troopers who were guarding the area.

'It makes their job easier,' she said. 'Though some have shown enterprise.'

The birds glanced at the neighbouring buildings and the people who'd scrambled onto windowsills and roofs to get the best possible view. Several ravens were perched amongst them and were communicating with each other in their distinctive, rasping calls.

'To left?

'Naaah!'

'Watch, watch.'

'Yaaah!'

'They've been here since daybreak,' said General. 'Extra eyes have arrived since, and there are other patrols along Whitehall itself. They all have the descriptions you gave, but they've seen nothing so far, not even Smales.'

'The descriptions may not help,' Sioluc replied. 'Like every other man, and most of the women, Prince Charles and Richard Cheevely will be wearing hats, and perhaps other disguises too.'

'The nightingales sang right through the night,' General remembered. 'Corex need only give the command and help will fly in from miles around. If we need it.'

'Let's hope we don't,' said Sioluc as more ravens arrived. 'Remember we are actively *looking* for the prince and his friend. If *we* can't find them, it's not likely anyone will recognise them purely by chance. We must be prepared, but not too hasty. If we summon help too soon, or without foundation, we might cause panic in the crowd. Meantime we are doing what we can, and I must go to His Majesty.'

Outside St. James's Palace, a dozen Parliamentarian guards were stamping their feet and swinging their arms to keep warm.

Sioluc flew past them and then twice round the

building, where she paused at various of its windows in the hope of spotting Edmund Smales. But it was to no avail. Nor did she see Mignonne or the children. They lived at Syon House now, and Sioluc had heard that the mood at St. James's was much the worse for their absence.

When the king emerged from the palace, the guards shuffled into blocks in front of and behind him, and Sioluc swooped down to the sparkling, frost-covered grass.

The king paused and looked at her curiously and she raised her right leg so he could see her diamond bracelet.

'What, bird? Have you come to bid me farewell?' he laughed. 'Let's walk together then. It is so cold today that I have two shirts on. I cannot be seen to shiver, you see, lest they think I am afraid. But the air will do me good.'

Sioluc cawed and stretched her wings, then set out across St. James's Park with the king and his guards.

At the foot of the steps to Whitehall Palace, the king hesitated, took a deep breath and swept one arm ahead of him, towards the door.

'Will you not enter, bird?' he asked.

The last thing Sioluc wanted was to be parted from His Majesty, but neither could she risk being trapped inside the palace's extensive buildings or caught by one of its guards.

She tipped her head sideways and shook out her

feathers.

'You will not enter,' the king sighed resignedly.

Sioluc shook herself again and turned to fly away.

'Wait, bird!' said the king. 'I would I had thought to see you today. I might have brought you something precious. My ruby ring, perhaps.'

He held his hands in front of him and spread his bare fingers.

'As it is...'

He reached under his hat and tugged sharply at his hair.

'Take this,' he said.

Sioluc gently took the lock of hair in her bill.

'Farewell, good loyal friend,' the king added. 'Farewell.'

Then he disappeared inside the palace.

As she flew back to the scaffold, Sioluc spotted a mistle thrush. She landed beside the bird and raised her right leg. The mistle thrush bowed.

'Carry this to the Tower,' Sioluc cawed as she passed the king's gift into the thrush's beak. 'Make sure to give it to Corex himself. Ask him to take care of it for me.'

Back on the scaffold, General had two pieces of news.

'They can't find an executioner,' he said. 'No one is willing.'

'That's hardly surprising,' Sioluc answered. 'But it does give us time.'

'We don't need it. Swithin thinks he's seen Cheevely

216

and the prince. He's been keeping an eye on them.'

'Where's Swithin now?' Sioluc asked.

'On the roof opposite.'

'Come over here, Swithin,' Sioluc called. 'What have you seen?'

'Maybe nothing,' Swithin replied as he landed beside her. 'But look there, in the crowd. Do you see the black horse with a white blaze? To the left of it is a stooped fellow. He's barely lifted his head since he got here.'

Sioluc followed the tilt of Swithin's bill.

'Next to him's another young man,' Swithin added. 'See how upright he stands? You can see his face very clearly, even from under his hat.'

'We have found them at last,' said Sioluc. 'The stooped fellow is almost certainly Prince Charles. The other is definitely Richard Cheevely.'

'What strange eyes he has,' Swithin remarked. 'Grey as a grey bird's plumage.'

Sioluc opened her beak to speak, but stopped short. When she finally said something, her voice was hoarse, hardly more than a whisper.

'What did you say?' she asked.

'I said grey. Like a pigeon. Or a gull, perhaps. Some such.'

General and Sioluc exchanged glances. They were both remembering their leader's words of warning.

'Their allegiance is worthless and often brief. For if the tide of fortune turns, they'll turn with it, and fly the other way.'

'No, Sioluc,' said General. 'You're wrong. It doesn't

217

apply to people, and anyway it's not possible. Cheevely is a trusted servant, a good friend of the prince. He would not betray him.'

But General was already stretching his wings.

'Go!' Sioluc ordered him.

She turned to Swithin.

'Tell the rest of the patrol to keep their eyes fixed on the prince and Cheevely. Especially Cheevely,' she said hurriedly. 'I'll be back as soon as I can.'

'But what if...?

'They're recognised? I'm hoping that would have happened by now.'

She leapt from the scaffold.

'My worry is Cheevely. We must concentrate on him,' she called over her shoulder as she flew away. 'He won't do anything before an executioner's found. Only then will the die be cast!'

She circled the air several times to gather her thoughts and weigh up her options. Finally, she headed east, to Bishopsgate Street.

CHAPTER THIRTY-SIX
A few minutes later

The Green Dragon was virtually deserted, but Edmund
Smales was there. He was slumped over the counter with
a pot of ale in one hand and another lined up ready and
waiting. As Sioluc swooped through the tavern door,
Smales drained the first pot and raised the second to his
mouth.

'To the king!' he slurred.

Sioluc landed beside him.

'Here's our bird again,' said the taverner's wife.
'Come for a bowl of something.'

'Ooh. Goo'day bird,' Smales spluttered.

The taverner's wife reached under the counter and
produced the scrap bowl, but Sioluc ignored it and leapt
onto Smales's shoulder.

He brushed her away.

She leapt again, this time onto his head, where she
scraped at his scalp with her talons.

'Geroff!' Smales flailed.

Sioluc tried a different tactic.

She hopped onto the counter, stretched out her right
leg and tapped her beak against her bracelet.

Smales blinked at the noise and shook his head as if to clear it. Sioluc bent her neck sideways and stared straight into his eyes.

'What ails thee, bird?' he asked.

Sioluc was clawing at his sleeve when he suddenly stood up, knocked his stool to the floor with a crash, and ran for the tavern door.

'Have you seen them?' he shouted. 'Where are they? Can you take me there?'

He was running fast now, streaming along Bishopsgate.

'They did not meet with Cripps, you know,' he added as Sioluc darted and swooped ahead of him, 'where are they, bird?'

He followed Sioluc until he realised where she was heading, then stopped dead in his tracks.

'The Banqueting House,' he panted. 'Don't tell me they're in the crowd!'

Sioluc gaped her beak.

'Gad's teeth!' Smales exclaimed. 'Are they gone mad?'

He began running again, and kept running until he could see the facade of The Banqueting House. Then he slowed to a saunter. The outermost circle of Roundhead troopers were sitting with their backs to him, their horses' hindquarters white with siftings of snow.

Sioluc hovered whilst Smales scanned the men from behind.

'I must find someone I know,' he mumbled to himself.

Eventually his eyes settled on the rider of a large bay.

'Nathaniel Starr,' he exhaled.

He walked forward and tapped Starr on the thigh. The trooper jumped and laid his hand on the hilt of his sword, but then recognised Smales. He smiled, allowed Smales to push past him, and told the trooper ahead of him to do the same.

Like this, the Parliamentarian 'mole' burrowed his way through the bank of guards and into the crowd. Sioluc stayed close to him until he'd spotted Prince Charles and Richard Cheevely and given her a quick, almost imperceptible nod. Then she returned to the scaffold, where Swithin and General were waiting.

'All done,' General told her. 'I spoke to Corex in person. He's on his way.'

'Good,' Sioluc replied. 'And now we have Smales to help us, too. I found him drowning his sorrows at The Green Dragon.'

She glanced up.

More ravens had arrived on the roofs of the surrounding buildings. They were passing constant signals to one another.

'Smaaales!'

'Yaaah!'

'Keepin' an eye?'

'Yaaah!'

'Prince an' Cheevely?'

'Yaaah!'

Four hours had elapsed since the king's arrival at The Palace of Whitehall. Now two men appeared at the window of The Banqueting House, both wearing masks and false beards. An executioner and assistant had been found at last, and they didn't want to be recognised.

Sioluc prayed that the men were properly trained and that their axe was razor sharp. Death by axe was a terrifying prospect, and needed to be swiftly done by an expert. Far too many beheadings were bodged.

Her own great-great-grandfather had been a Raven Ambassador, just like her. Also just like her, he had had bestowed on him the honourable but unpleasant task of witnessing the death of a monarch. It had happened at Fotheringhay Castle in Scotland, and the monarch had been Mary, Queen of Scots, future grandmother of King Charles himself.

Mary had also died by the axe. Her executioner had taken three blows to do the job, and the queen's lips had still been moving fifteen minutes after the last. Her little dog had later been found hiding amongst her skirts and clinging to her body. At least King Charles's dog could not do that, and for the first time ever, Sioluc was glad that Cavendish was dead.

King Charles's executioner stepped onto the scaffold and examined the block, then disappeared inside again. On the other side of the street, another four ravens landed.

Sioluc looked to the east. The sky was swirling with birds. Sideways-on they were like a smattering of tiny ink spots, but when they turned they became a vast, manta-like cloud. Twist, turn. The same thing was happening to the south. Buildings obscured Sioluc's view to north and west, but it didn't matter. She could hear them, and they numbered thousands.

The crowd had also noticed the preponderance of birds. People were pointing to the sky and staring at the rows of ravens along the gutters and ridges.

Corex was amongst them, now. He was sitting slightly apart from the others, on the apex of a stone pediment. His body was tipped forward and his head was cocked sideways, his steely black eyes not missing a trick.

The executioner and his assistant returned. This time they were carrying the axe.

The king appeared at the window and then stepped onto the scaffold.

He asked the executioner what he should do with his hair.

More birds landed.

'We might not need them,' said General tentatively.

'I hope not,' Sioluc replied.

The king tucked his hair under a cap. He removed his cloak and unbuttoned his doublet. He asked if the block could be raised so that he might kneel rather than lie down. The executioner said 'no'.

Several miles away, at Syon House, Princess Elizabeth was sitting by the fireside staring at the flames and plucking miserably at a tear-soaked handkerchief. Lying at her feet was Mignonne. The little dog hadn't thought about Richard Cheevely in months. Now she couldn't stop. She could see him very clearly, as though he was standing right in front of her. His pale grey eyes were shining.

Sioluc could see Cheevely too. He was still standing in the crowd, still shoulder to shoulder with Prince Charles. The prince was still noticeably hunched, with his chin resting on his chest and his face almost completely obscured by his hat, but Cheevely was bolt upright, chin up, grey eyes sparkling.

'So what?' thought Sioluc. 'There is no one here to recognise him. He doesn't need to disguise himself. Perhaps I am wrong, after all.'

Corex flew down from the pediment and settled himself beside Sioluc and General.

The king began to pray.

Mignonne jumped from Elizabeth's lap and gazed at the ceiling.

The executioner asked for the king's forgiveness, and raised the axe.

Sioluc couldn't watch.

She heard the swish of the blade, the thud of the blessedly swift and single blow, and the gasp from the crowd. That was enough. Her duty as witness was done. She had no desire to see the king's head roll from his body.

The executioner bent to retrieve the head and hold it up.

Mignonne slumped to the floor and howled.

The crowd groaned, then fell silent.

Sioluc, intent on Richard Cheevely, saw a flicker in the grey eyes, and suddenly knew, utterly and unquestionably, what he was about to do.

'The King is dead!' Cheevely cried. 'An' I 'ave 'ere beside me 'is son! An'...'

Mignonne barked.

'Now!' Sioluc squawked. 'Now!'

Corex and General made straight for Richard Cheevely. Whatever anybody had heard or thought when he'd spoken was swiftly forgotten. The cold, exhausted crowd had little remaining spirit as it was, and the birds' terrifying black wings and tautly stretched, iron-taloned feet quickly forced a clear, sacrificial space around their hapless, flailing target.

Meanwhile, the other birds; not just ravens, but rooks, crows, jackdaws, starlings, blackbirds and thrushes were swooping from the roofs and swirling from the skies. Some scattered the throngs of people lining Whitehall, driving them back and clearing the way for those who would soon be caught in a stampede from Banqueting House. Others choreographed that very stampede. They went for the troopers guarding the scaffold. They screeched, gaped their beaks and raked with their talons until the horses broke rank, and the crowd clambered over one another to reach the comparative safety of Whitehall.

In the midst of it all was Prince Charles, who was

buffeted and jostled and carried haphazardly along with the panicking mass. He must have felt very alone. He certainly didn't notice, amongst all the screaming and flapping of people and birds, that one particular raven was spinning and rolling above his head. Nor did he see how Edmund Smales kept sight of Sioluc's unwavering mark until he could push his way through to the shocked, pale-faced prince and take him firmly by the arm.

With Sioluc still guiding them, Smales and Prince Charles hung back and filtered into the tail end of the crowd. The Roundhead horses had settled by then and, though dispersed, the troopers were still a threat. But Smales and the prince knew how to keep their heads down, and they soon reached the relative safety of St. James's Park.

They collapsed, panting, on the grass and Sioluc landed beside them.

'Was it Cheevely's idea to stay here, not to meet with Cripps?' Smales asked breathlessly.

Prince Charles sniffed and wiped his nose on his sleeve.

'Yes,' he replied, his voice caught in his throat. 'Yes, it was.'

Smales shook his head.

'I should have gone with you,' he said in a tone loaded with regret. 'I should have seen you to Cripps's boat, but the meeting I had...well, we needed to examine every last option. We sat up all night. Every one of us was prepared to die. In the end we realised it would be futile. It would only have prolonged things. There was nothing more we could do. We could not save your father.'

'No,' Prince Charles replied. 'No one could.'

Smales sighed.

'Tell me, Sire,' he eventually asked. 'How did you find Cheevely? I mean, this is *London*. It's a big place at the best of times. But after six years of *war*? People are scattered, old addresses have been burned down or boarded up. You told me he'd corresponded with you...'

'No,' Charles replied.

'No?'

'No. I haven't heard from him for nearly three years. Not since the night I sailed for The Scillies.'

Smales took a deep breath.

'So how did you find him?' he asked wearily.

'I didn't. He found me.'

'In other words,' said Smales, 'he knew you were coming to London. He knew you were coming, Charles! What does that say to you?'

'That somebody tailed me here,' said Prince Charles miserably.

'Tailed you and handed you over to Cheevely,' Smales confirmed.

'Cheevely,' Prince Charles repeated. 'Of *all* people. I cannot credit it, yet he gave me away. He could have done it earlier, you know. I sent him on an errand to fetch you. He could have given me over then, but he didn't. Why is that, do you think?'

Smales put a comforting arm around the prince's shoulder.

'Because he was out for glory?' he suggested. 'He

wanted to do it in public so people would know about it. As to why he did it at all, we may never find out. Perhaps something happened to his family at the hands of the Royalists, perhaps he was simply a bad apple. But you are safe. That's what matters. We must get you some lodgings for tonight, and by morning we'll have you out of them again and back across The Channel.'

'Elizabeth?' Prince Charles inquired.

'Is at Syon house. Henry too. They are well. They have Mignonne.'

'Ah, little Mignonne,' the Prince whispered tearfully. 'She will be of comfort to them. I'm glad of that.'

'You will return, Sire. You *will* return one day. You *will* be king.'

The Prince smiled wanly.

'King Charles the Second,' he whispered.

228

CHAPTER THIRTY-SEVEN
Bo's House.
The 21st Century

'Cheevely was never seen again,' said Cavendish. 'Corex and General prodded and stabbed at him until they'd harried him far away from The Banqueting House and he fell down in the snow.'

'Did they kill him?' asked Bo.

'No.'

'They should have. They had the weapons and the motive.'

'They certainly did,' Cavendish replied. 'But killing people isn't part of raven lore. They left that to Smales, and Smales certainly did his best to hunt Cheevely down. But it was not to be. Smales gave up after a while and followed Prince Charles to Holland. When Charles returned to England...'

'He did?'

'Yes, of course he did!' Cavendish exclaimed. 'He became King Charles II. Didn't you know that?'

'No,' said Bo. 'Why would I?'

'Well, he did,' Cavendish replied. 'It took a while, but when Charles finally came home, Smales came too. He worked for King Charles for years after that, but turned down all offers to be admitted to court. He preferred The Green Dragon.'

'And Old Sowerbutts?' Bo asked. 'What happened to him?'

'Oh, him,' said Cavendish with a sneer. 'He went on tending the palace gardens. Cromwell had taken them over by then, and Sowerbutts really *was* old. He died more peacefully than he deserved.'

'I never asked you about the pony dog. He must have died, too. He was already doddery when I met him.'

'The pony dog? Who's the pony dog?'

'You know. The big dog from the portrait. Smales took us for a walk together the first time I went back, but then I never saw him again.'

'That was Mansion,' Cavendish smiled. 'Sweet, slobbery Mansion. He died at Windsor Castle. That's where he lived, really. He'd only come up to London to be in the portrait.'

Bo hesitated. She wasn't sure she wanted to hear the answer to her next question.

'Elizabeth and Henry?'

Cavendish turned away.

'...were taken to Carisbrooke Castle,' he sighed.

'Elizabeth was never very strong...' offered Bo.

She knew the news was bad.

'I'm sorry, Bo. It was just too much for her. She got soaked in a shower of rain one day. It gave her a fever. She may have had tuberculosis before then, but whatever the reason, she died in her sleep.'

'Mignonne was with her,' Bo said in a sudden rush. 'She stayed on at Carisbrooke with Henry but one night she just slipped away, too.'

'Sioluc died at that same instant,' interjected Cavendish. 'The ravens buried her at the Tower of London with full honours, and Mignonne was laid to rest beside Elizabeth.'

'Poor Elizabeth.'

'Yes. She had a short, sad life.'

'Mignonne and Sioluc had *wonderful* lives,' said Bo wistfully. 'I was lucky to be able to see that. Thank you, Cavendish. Thank you for showing me those wonderful lives.'

'My pleasure,' Cavendish replied.

EPILOGUE

'Bo?'

'Yes?'

'What are you thinking?'

'Oh, you know, just about Mignonne and Sioluc. And how nice it is sitting here with you, being Bo again, doing Bo things.'

Cavendish rested his head on his paws and tried to pull his thoughts together. Then he spoke again, very slowly and deliberately.

'Perhaps now is a good time to tell you something,' he began cautiously.

'Go on,' urged Bo.

'I think you may have a very special gift.'

'Oh, I know,' Bo chirruped. 'That's how I'm here beside you, how I could go back to being Mignonne, how I could be Sioluc the raven.'

'No, I mean a *really* special gift. Going back to a life that was once yours is one thing. Becoming Sioluc as well was extraordinary...'

'But?'

'But I believe you can do even more. I believe you can choose any poodle or poodle ancestor and become that dog. If I'm right, then the world of time travel is your oyster.'

'*Any* poodle?'

'Any.'

'Wow!'

'Indeed.'

'The trouble is,' said Bo sadly, 'I don't know about other places and times. So how would I choose where to go?'

'That *is* difficult,' Cavendish replied. 'But don't worry. I'll help you.'

Then Bo suddenly had her own idea.

'I know!' she exclaimed. 'What about my namesake? Might she have had a poodle?'

'Your namesake? *Bo*? Who was called Bo?'

'Not Bo. That's my pet name. My real name's Boadicea. She was some sort of queen, wasn't she?'

'In Roman Britain,' Cavendish nodded. 'Have you any idea what life was like then?'

'No,' said Bo meekly. 'I've just told you that.'

'It was very grim,' the spaniel said. 'Really horrid. People painted their faces blue and wore animal skins. Go back there and you'll probably end up as someone's skirt. Even Boadicea couldn't stand it. She poisoned herself in the end. And I doubt she ever saw anything even remotely resembling a poodle. If she had she'd probably have eaten it. But poodles are a very ancient breed. There are Roman and Greek coins with pictures of dogs just like you on them. So you *could* visit Roman times, but you should at least aim for somewhere civilised. How about Egypt? Alexandria was a beautiful place.'

'Did it have a queen?' Bo asked.

'It most certainly did. One of the most famous ever.'

'Did she have a poodle?

'If anyone did, it was her.'

'Did she wear furry skirts?'

'No,' said Cavendish. 'She didn't need to. Her country was hot and sunny.'

'Sounds lovely,' said Bo dully.

Cavendish looked exasperated.

'Don't knock me over in the rush,' he said.

'Sorry,' Bo replied. 'It's just that it all seems so foreign, and such a long time ago.'

'Isn't that the point? Give it a try, Bo. If you don't like it, you can come straight back here. We'll find somewhere less taxing for you. Rainy Newcastle on a mid-Victorian Monday, perhaps.'

'Very funny.'

'Look. I don't even know if we can get you to Egypt. So let's just see, shall we?' Cavendish suggested. 'If you choose something from the here and now, it will clear your mind and help you concentrate.'

He tipped his head.

'What about that?' he suggested.

Bo looked up.

Scrambling repeatedly up the wall of the coal hole was a large black beetle. It was about three centimetres long and had a pair of fearsome looking jaws.

'Grief! What's *that*?'

'A stag beetle. Otherwise known as a scarab. They're

quite rare here nowadays. Take it as a sign.'

'A sign of what?' Bo asked.

'That Egypt is the place to go. The Egyptians worshipped scarab beetles.'

'Really?' Bo shuddered. 'Then I want to go somewhere else.'

'Give it a try, Bo,' Cavendish pleaded. 'Think of Egypt.'

'Why are you so keen on this place?' asked Bo suspiciously. 'And how can I think of it when I've never been there?'

'I'll help you. Close your eyes. Remember the stag beetle?'

Bo nodded.

'Yes' she said. 'I can see it in my head. Unfortunately.'

'Good,' said Cavendish. 'Now imagine a place of sandy deserts and lush green wheat fields. There are palm trees and a great river, the longest in the world. You live by the sea, where the breezes are scented with spices, rich soil and exotic flowers....'

'Hold up!' said Bo.

'What now?'

'You'd better tell me what this queen was called. So I can recognise her.'

Cavendish chuckled.

'I don't think you'll be in any doubt,' he replied. 'You'll know her when you see her.'

'Just in case.'

'Cleopatra. Her name was Cleopatra of Egypt.'

The story of Bo's adventures in Egypt
will be told in her next book

MORTAL GODS

www.bothepoodle.co.uk

PEOPLE AND PLACES IN STORM DOGS

The dates and descriptions in this book are based on historical fact, as are the characters and locations. Here's what became of them all:

(The) Banqueting House, where King Charles was executed, survived the destruction of Whitehall Palace, (see below), and is open to visitors.

Bedford House, where Hetty-Anne was born, was demolished in around 1770 and replaced by a Georgian crescent, also subsequently demolished.

Carisbrooke Castle on the Isle of Wight is partly ruined but is open to the public. It is a fascinating, atmospheric place, and has exhibits relating to King Charles's imprisonment. Both of his bedrooms can be seen. The first is intact. The second has lost its roof and floor, but its fireplace and the window from which he tried to escape are still visible, high up on the north wall.

Cavalier King Charles Spaniels are today's equivalent of Cavendish. The breed that was familiar to Kings Charles I and II almost died out during Victorian times, when smaller, more pug-like dogs became fashionable. These were called King Charles Spaniels, but in 1928 people began to look at old portraits from the 16th, 17th and 18th Centuries to see if they could recreate something more akin to the original. The result was the longer nosed, and taller, Cavalier.

King Charles I was beheaded on the afternoon of 30th January 1649. He is buried at St. George's Chapel, Windsor.

Prince Charles lived in exile from 1646. There is no record of him ever having attempted to visit his father after that. In 1660, Charles returned to England, where he was crowned King Charles II in 1661. He ruled until he died in 1685. The people called him The Merry Monarch because his reign was a huge and welcome contrast to the bleak Cromwellian years. It was also overshadowed by the Great Plague of 1665 and the Great Fire of London in 1666, which Charles himself helped to fight. Charles was devoted to a particular type of spaniel and often owned several at a time which followed him everywhere. The breed was eventually named after him (see above). Charles was charming, courteous and courageous, though also rather devious. He had many children but no legitimate heirs.

Oliver Cromwell ruled England as Lord Protector until his death in 1658. This break from monarchy was a good thing in some ways, and helped make Britain and her constitution what they are today. But whilst Cromwell's legacy is valuable to us, his rule became increasingly dictatorial. He imposed harsh, puritanical laws but failed to do many of the good things he'd promised. He wore a cloak embroidered with gold and even considered becoming king. He was certainly as guilty as the king had been when it came to ignoring Parliament. Cromwell was initially buried in Westminster Abbey, but in 1661 his body was exhumed and he was hanged as a traitor at Tyburn (now Marble Arch) in London. His head was then removed and displayed at Westminster Hall for nearly 20 years.

Sir Anthony Van Dyck was born in Antwerp. He became a hugely prolific, successful and influential portrait painter, and died in London in December 1641.

Edgehill is now a protected battle site. It is free to visit and is said to be haunted. A small museum at Farnborough House, near Banbury, contains items from the battle.

Princess Elizabeth was moved to Carisbrooke Castle in August 1650, and died there the following month. She is buried at Newport parish church on the Isle of Wight, where a monument was erected in her memory on the orders of Queen Victoria.

Colonel Robert Hammond left the Isle of Wight in 1654 for a posting in Dublin. He died a short time later.

William Harvey was physician to both King James I and VI, and King Charles I. Harvey discovered that it is the heart which pumps blood around the body, and also concluded that bleeding slows down in cold weather. He nursed Van Dyck during the painter's last illness, was present at the Battle of Edgehill, and died in 1657 at the age of 79.

Princess Hetty-Anne was always a favourite of her brother, the future Charles II. He and their father visited her at Exeter shortly after the queen had fled. Hetty-Anne was smuggled to France in 1646 and later married the brother of Louis XIV. She corresponded with Charles throughout her life, and died near Paris in 1670. Some people think she was poisoned.

Queen Henrietta Maria never really recovered from her husband's death, and dressed in black for the rest of her life. She came back to England for visits after her son was crowned Charles II, but always returned to France, where she died in 1669.

Prince Henry was taken to Carisbrooke Castle in 1650 and remained alone there after the death of his sister, Princess Elizabeth. In 1653, Henry was given permission to go abroad. He returned to England when his brother Charles was restored as king, but caught smallpox and died shortly afterwards.

Hurst Castle is situated on The Solent in Hampshire.

The original building is Tudor, but over the years it has been much extended to defend the English coast.

Prince James succeeded his brother (Charles II), in 1685 and became James II, but was driven from the throne in 1688. He was replaced by his daughter Mary and her husband, William. James died in France in 1701.

Princess Mary was the oldest daughter of Charles I, and married the Prince of Orange when she was ten. She returned to England when her brother, Charles, was restored to the throne, but died of smallpox a short time later. From 1689 her son, William, ruled England with his wife and cousin (daughter of Prince James), who was also called Mary.

Sir John Mennes was a sea admiral for both King Charles I, who knighted him, and King Charles II, who made him Comptroller of the Navy. He captained The Lion and took Henrietta-Maria and Princess Mary to Holland. Mennes died in London in 1671.

Poodles were popular pets of the time and can be seen in many of its paintings. Prince Rupert really did have a poodle named Boy, which sat on his saddle before battle. Rupert was devastated when Boy was killed in 1644 at the Battle of Marston Moor, one of the bloodiest of the war. Another of Rupert's dogs, probably a Labrador type, was captured by Parliamentarians and had its ears cut off to make it a 'Roundhead.'

Portrait of the Five Eldest Children of King Charles I by Anthony Van Dyck. The original can be seen in The Queen's Ballroom at Windsor Castle.

Portrait of Prince Rupert (as a boy) by Anthony Van Dyck is now in the Kunsthistorisches Museum, Vienna.

Prince Rupert lived in exile in Europe until Charles II became king. He then returned to England where he later became Constable of Windsor Castle. He was fascinated by science and may have invented the technique for mezzotint engraving. He became rather fierce in later life, even King Charles II was apprehensive of him. Rupert died at his house in London in 1682.

St James's Palace is still an official royal residence and is the London home of Princess Anne and Princess Alexandra. Its complex includes Clarence House, London home of The Prince of Wales, Prince William and Prince Harry, plus many royal offices and State rooms. It is not open to the public.

The Tower of London is open to the public and remains much as it was at the time. The White Tower still stands, though other buildings, notably the Great Hall, which was roofless even in King Charles's time, have disappeared. Ravens have always lived at The Tower, and still do. Legend has it that if they ever leave, it will collapse. The Tower has many exhibits from King Charles's time, including the back and breast plates worn by Prince

Charles at the Battle of Edgehill. The famous Crown Jewels are comparatively new. They were made for the coronation of Charles II because the previous regalia had been melted down or sold by Cromwell.

Westminster Hall has a brass tablet marking the spot where the king sat during his trial. The hall is one of the few buildings to have survived a fire that destroyed the original Palace of Westminster in 1834. The current Palace of Westminster, which includes the Hall and the Houses of Parliament, is open to the public.

Mrs Wheeler was the king's laundress and smuggled letters for him at Carisbrooke. She probably lived to a ripe old age.

(The Palace of) Whitehall was destroyed by fire in 1698 but the Banqueting House survived.

Richard Cheevely, Old Sowerbutts and Edmund Smales are fictitious names. They were spies, after all, so who knows what they were really called?

DATES

1599	25 April	**Birth** of Oliver Cromwell
1600	19 November	**Birth** of King Charles 1
1625	27 March	**Accession** of King Charles 1
	11 May	**Marriage** of King Charles 1 to Henrietta Maria
1630	29 May	**Birth** of Prince Charles
1631	04 November	**Birth** of Princess Mary
1633	14 October	**Birth** of Prince James
1635	29 December	**Birth** of Princess Elizabeth
1636	17 March	**Birth** of Princess Anne
1640	08 July	**Birth** of Prince Henry
	November	**Death** of Princess Anne
1641	09 December	**Death** of Sir Anthony Van Dyck, in London
1642	23 February	**Departure** of the queen and Princess Mary from Dover
	23 October	**Battle** of Edgehill
1643	22 February	**Return** of Queen Henrietta Maria from Holland to Yorkshire

1643 13 July	**Reunion** of the king and queen, near Oxford
1644 January	**Warning** from John Williams in a letter about Oliver Cromwell
17 April	**Departure** of the queen from Oxford to Exeter
16 June	**Birth** of Princess Henriette-Anne
02 July	**Battle** of Marston Moor and **Death** of Rupert's poodle, Boy
1645 14 June	**Battle** of Naseby
1646 02 March	**Escape** of Prince Charles to the Scilly Isles
16 April	**Escape** of Prince Charles to Jersey
27 April	**Meeting** with the Scots - the king sets out
25 June	**Escape** of Prince Charles to France
	Capture of Oxford, Prince Rupert and Prince James
25 July	**Escape** of Princess Henriette-Anne to France
1647 February	**Arrival** of King Charles, now in Parliament's hands, at Holdenby
03 June	**Removal** of King Charles by Cromwell to Childerley
03 July	**Removal** of King Charles to Caversham
15 July	**Meeting** of Princess Elizabeth, Prince James, Prince Henry, their father and Cromwell at The Greyhound Inn, Maidenhead
12 August	**Removal** of King Charles to Oatlands (and then to Hampton Court Palace)